The ki

Stories + stories

RE THE

KINGFISHER
An imprint of Kingfisher Publications Plc
New Penderel House, 283-288 High Holborn
London WC1V 7HZ
www.kingfisherpub.com

First published by Kingfisher 1997
This edition published by Kingfisher 2005
2 4 6 8 10 9 7 5 3

A CIP catalogue record for this book is available from the British Library.

ISBN 0 7534 1161 X
2TR/0705/THOM/FR(MA)/115WF

Printed in India

Acknowledgements

The publisher would like to thank the copyright holders for permission to reproduce the following copyright material:

Joan Aiken: A M Heath & Co. Ltd for Chapter 1 from *Arabel's Raven* by Joan Aiken, British Broadcasting Corporation
1972. Copyright © Joan Aiken Enterprises Ltd. **Malorie Blackman**: Victor Gollancz Ltd for "Rescuing the Rescuers" from
Girl Wonder and the Terrific Twins by Malorie Blackman, Victor Gollancz Ltd 1991. Copyright © Oneta Malorie Blackman
1991. **Judy Blume**: The Bodley Head Children's Books for "Dribble" from *Tales of a Fourth Grade Nothing* by Judy Blume,
The Bodley Head 1979. Copyright © Judy Blume 1972. **Betsy Byars**: The Bodley Head Children's Books for "E!G!G!S!"
from *The Moon and Me* by Betsy Byars, The Bodley Head 1993. Copyright © Betsy Byars 1991. **Italo Calvino**: "The
Parrot" from *Italian Folktales: Selected and retold by Italo Calvino*, translated by George Martin (Penguin Books 1982, first
published in Italy by Giulio Einaudi Editore, s.p.a., as *Fiabe Italiane* 1956) copyright Giulio Einaudi Editore, s.p.a.,1956.
This translation copyright © Harcourt Brace Jovanovich Inc., 1980. Reproduced by permission of Penguin Books Ltd.
Barbee Oliver Carleton: The author for "The Pretend Pony" from *More Bedtime Stories to Read Aloud* by Barbee Oliver
Carleton, Golden Pleasure Books 1963. Copyright © Barbee Oliver Carleton. **Beverly Cleary**: Text excerpt, "Henry's
Canine Teeth" from *Henry and Ribsy* by Beverly Cleary. Copyright © 1954 by Beverly Cleary. By permission of Morrow
Junior Books, a division of William Morrow & Company, Inc. **Helen Cresswell**: The Bodley Head Children's Books for
"Posy Bates Goes Green" from *Meet Posy Bates* by Helen Cresswell, The Bodley Head 1990. Copyright © Helen Cresswell
1990. **Meindert DeJong**: The Lutterworth Press for "A Barn is a Daytime Place" from *Puppy Summer* by Meindert DeJong,
Lutterworth Press 1966. Copyright © Meindert DeJong 1966. **Ted Hughes**: Faber and Faber Ltd for "How the Cat
Became" from *How the Whale Became* by Ted Hughes, Faber and Faber Ltd 1963. Copyright © Ted Hughes 1963.
Dick King-Smith: Victor Gollancz Ltd for "What a Dear Little Thing!" from *Martin's Mice* by Dick King-Smith, Victor
Gollancz Ltd 1988. Copyright © Dick King-Smith 1988. **Margaret Mahy**: The Orion Publishing Group Ltd for "Mrs
Bartelmy's Pet" from *The Second Margaret Mahy Story Book* by Margaret Mahy, J M Dent & Sons Ltd 1973. Copyright ©
Margaret Mahy 1973. **Liss Norton**: The author for "A Pet Fit for a King" by Liss Norton. Copyright © Liss Norton 1997.
Ursula Moray Williams: "House Mouse" reproduced with permission of Curtis Brown Ltd, London on behalf of Ursula
Moray Williams. Copyright © Ursula Moray Williams 1990. **David Henry Wilson**: Macmillan Children's Books for
"Heaven" from *Do Gerbils Go to Heaven?* by David Henry Wilson, Macmillan Children's Books 1996. Copyright © David
Henry Wilson 1996.

Every effort has been made to obtain permission to reproduce copyright material but there may be cases where we have
been unable to trace a copyright holder. The publisher will be happy to correct any omissions in future printings.

THE KINGFISHER TREASURY OF

Pet Stories

CHOSEN BY SUZANNE CARNELL
ILLUSTRATED BY MICHAEL REID

KINGFISHER

CONTENTS

7 How the Cat Became
TED HUGHES

15 Henry's Canine Teeth
BEVERLY CLEARY

26 The Pretend Pony
BARBEE OLIVER CARLETON

32 Dribble
JUDY BLUME

48 A Pet Fit for a King
LISS NORTON

57 Rescuing the Rescuers
MALORIE BLACKMAN

64 Arabel's Raven
JOAN AIKEN

76 Heaven
DAVID HENRY WILSON

88   Posy Bates Goes Green
       HELEN CRESSWELL

105   Mrs Bartelmy's Pet
       MARGARET MAHY

110   The Parrot
       An Italian folktale by ITALO CALVINO

119   House-Mouse
       URSULA MORAY WILLIAMS

125   E!G!G!S!
       BETSY BYARS

133   The Duke Who Had Too Many Giraffes
       FIONA MACDONALD

143   What a Dear Little Thing!
       DICK KING-SMITH

151   A Barn is a Daytime Place
       MEINDERT DeJONG

HOW THE CAT BECAME

Ted Hughes

Things were running very smoothly and most of the creatures were highly pleased with themselves. Lion was already famous. Even the little shrews and moles and spiders were pretty well known.

But among all these busy creatures there was one who seemed to be getting nowhere. It was Cat.

Cat was a real oddity. The others didn't know what to make of him at all.

He lived in a hollow tree in the wood. Every night, when the rest of the creatures were sound asleep, he retired to the depths of his tree – then such sounds, such screechings, yowlings, wailings! The bats that slept upside-down all day long in the hollows of the tree branches awoke with a start and fled with their wing-tips stuffed into their ears. It seemed to them that Cat was having the worst nightmares ever – ten at a time.

But no. Cat was tuning his violin. If only you could have seen him! Curled in the warm smooth hollow of his tree, gazing up through the hole at the top of the trunk, smiling at the stars, winking at the moon – his violin tucked under his chin. Ah, Cat was a happy one.

And all night long he sat there composing his tunes.

Now the creatures didn't like this at all. They saw no use in his music, it made no food, it built no nest, it didn't even keep him warm. And the way Cat lounged around all day, sleeping in the sun, was just more than they could stand.

"He's a bad example," said Beaver, "he never does a stroke of work! What if our children think they can live as idly as he does?"

"It's time," said Weasel, "that Cat had a job like everybody else in the world."

So the creatures of the wood formed a Committee to persuade Cat to take a job.

Jay, Magpie and Parrot went along at dawn and sat in the topmost twigs of Cat's old tree. As soon as Cat poked his head out, they all began together:

"You've to get a job. Get a job! Get a job!"

That was only the beginning of it. All day long, everywhere he went, those birds were at him:

"Get a job! Get a job!"

And try as he would, Cat could not get one wink of sleep.

That night he went back to his tree early. He was far too tired to practise on his violin and fell fast asleep in a few minutes. Next morning, when he poked his head out of the tree at first light, the three birds of the Committee were there again, loud as ever:

"Get a job!"

Cat ducked back down into his tree and began to think. He wasn't going to start grubbing around in the wet woods all day, as they wanted him to. Oh no. He wouldn't have any time to play his violin if he did that. There was only one thing to do and he did it.

He tucked his violin under his arm and suddenly jumped out at the top of the tree and set off through the woods at a run. Behind him, shouting and calling, came Jay, Magpie and Parrot.

Other creatures that were about their daily work in the undergrowth looked up when Cat ran past. No one had ever seen Cat run before.

"Cat's up to something," they called to each other. "Maybe he's going to get a job at last."

Deer, Wild Boar, Bear, Ferret, Mongoose, Porcupine and a cloud of birds set off after Cat to see where he was going.

After a great deal of running they came to the edge of the forest. There they stopped. As they peered through the leaves they looked sideways at each other and trembled. Ahead of them, across an open field covered with haycocks, was Man's farm.

But Cat wasn't afraid. He went straight on, over the field, and up to Man's door. He raised his paw and banged as hard as he could in the middle of the door.

Man was so surprised to see Cat that at first he just stood, eyes wide, mouth open. No creature ever dared to come on to his fields, let alone knock at his door. Cat spoke first.

"I've come for a job," he said.

"A job?" asked Man, hardly able to believe his ears.

"Work," said Cat. "I want to earn my living."

Man looked him up and down, then saw his long claws.

"You look as if you'd make a fine rat-catcher," said Man.

Cat was surprised to hear that. He wondered what it was about him that made him look like a rat-catcher. Still, he wasn't going to miss the chance of a job. So he stuck out his chest and said: "Been doing it for years."

"Well then, I've a job for you," said Man. "My farm's swarming with rats and mice. They're in my haystacks, they're in my corn sacks, and they're all over the pantry."

So before Cat knew where he was, he had been signed on as a Rat-and-Mouse-Catcher. His pay was milk, and meat, and a place at the fireside. He slept all day and worked all night.

At first he had a terrible time. The rats pulled his tail, the mice nipped his ears. They climbed on to rafters above him and dropped down - thump!

on to him in the dark. They teased the life out of him.

But Cat was a quick learner. At the end of the week he could lay out a dozen rats and twice as many mice within half an hour. If he'd gone on laying them out all night there would pretty soon have been none left, and Cat would have been out of a job. So he just caught a few each night - in the first ten minutes or so. Then he retired into the barn and played his violin till morning. This was just the job he had been looking for.

Man was delighted with him. And Mrs Man thought he was beautiful. She took him on to her lap and stroked him for hours on end. What a life! thought Cat. If only those silly creatures in the dripping wet woods could see him now!

Well, when the other farmers saw what a fine rat-and-mouse-catcher Cat was, they all wanted cats too. Soon there were so many cats that our Cat decided to form a string band. Oh yes, they were all great violinists. Every night, after making one pile of rats and another of mice, each cat left his farm and was away over the fields to a little dark spinney.

Then what tunes! All night long ...

Pretty soon lady cats began to arrive. Now, every night, instead of just music, there was dancing too. And what dances! If only you could have crept up there and peeped into the glade from behind a tree

and seen the cats dancing – the glossy furred ladies and the tomcats, some pearly grey, some ginger red, and all with wonderful green flashing eyes. Up and down the glade, with the music flying out all over the night.

At dawn they hung their violins in the larch trees, dashed back to the farms, and pretended they had been working all night among the rats and mice. They lapped their milk hungrily, stretched out at the fireside, and fell asleep with smiles on their faces.

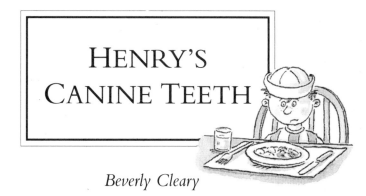

HENRY'S CANINE TEETH

Beverly Cleary

That evening, when Henry wore his sailor hat to the dinner table, he noticed his mother glance at him and then look at his father. She looked as if she was going to say something, but instead she sighed and was silent.

"You're looking pretty gloomy," remarked Mr Huggins, as he filled Henry's plate.

"Yeah," said Henry. "Don't give me much to eat. I'm not very hungry." Henry was careful to bite with his solid front teeth. He couldn't take chances with his loose teeth. He had to have them to show off to people who started making fun of his hair.

"I'm afraid the boys were giving him a bad time about his hair," exclaimed Mrs Huggins.

"Would you feel better if you went to the barber to see what he could do about it?" asked Henry's father. "A short crew cut might help."

15

"Well, maybe, but I don't think anything would help very much," said Henry. He wiggled first his right tooth and then his left tooth.

"I wonder if..." began Mrs Huggins and paused.

"If what?" Mr Huggins asked.

"Oh, nothing. I was just thinking." Mrs Huggins suddenly smiled at Henry.

Henry wiggled his teeth and wondered what his mother was thinking about. He hoped it wasn't anything like another home haircut.

"Really, Henry," said his mother, "you shouldn't go around with your teeth flapping that way."

"Aw, Mum, they don't flap," protested Henry. "They just wiggle."

"I see by the paper that old teeth left under pillows are turning into quarters instead of dimes because the cost of living has gone up," said Mr Huggins.

Henry grinned. He knew it was really his father who had always taken away his old teeth and left

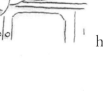

the dimes under his pillow. But right now, much as he could use two quarters, he needed two loose teeth more.

The next morning Henry examined his hair in the mirror. He could not see that it had grown at all, so he put on his sailor hat and moped around the house. He tried drawing a face on an electric-light bulb with coloured chalk. When he found the face did not shine through the shade the way he had planned, he felt even gloomier. He stood with his nose pressed against the front window pane until Ribsy scratched at the door and asked to be let out.

Henry followed his dog out of the door and sat down on the front steps. Gloomy as he felt about his hair, he didn't want to risk losing that fishing trip by giving Ribsy a chance to get into trouble with the neighbours. While he kept his eye on Ribsy, he could not keep from poking first his right tooth and then his left tooth with his tongue. They were looser all right. He discovered he could poke the two teeth out between his lips so they felt like little tusks.

As Henry experimented with his teeth, he happened to glance up Klickitat Street. Then, thinking he must be seeing things, he jumped up and stared. Robert and Scooter were walking towards him, both of them wearing sailor hats with the brims turned down over their eyebrows!

Well, how do you like that, thought Henry. Wearing sailor hats just to make fun of me. A couple of fine friends they turned out to be. Well, they weren't going to get a chance to tease him. "Come on, Ribsy," he said. "Let's go in the house before they see us."

Ribsy did not care to go into the house. He was busy sniffing the rosebushes along the edge of the Grumbies' property.

"O.K., you old dog," muttered Henry, and steeled himself for the meeting with Scooter and Robert.

Side by side the two boys walked down the street. They did not seem to see Henry. Looking straight ahead, they stalked past the Huggins' house.

Henry stared after them. What's the matter with them anyhow, he wondered. What did I do to them? Then a thought struck Henry. Could it be? No, it couldn't. Yes, it must be! Suddenly Henry had a feeling he was no longer the only boy with a chewed-up haircut. "Hey!" he yelled.

Robert and Scooter stalked on.

Why are they acting like that, Henry wondered. It's not my fault if they have home haircuts. Henry felt he had to know for sure. If he wasn't the only one with the chewed-up hair, things wouldn't be so bad. "Hey, fellows," he yelled again, and as he yelled his tongue touched one of his loose teeth. What were a couple of loose teeth anyhow? He made up his mind. "Want to watch me pull my teeth?"

Robert and Scooter hesitated. Then they stopped and turned round.

"I've thought of a good way to pull them," said Henry, trying frantically to think of an unusual way to get those teeth out of his mouth.

"How?" demanded Scooter, as he and Robert came up to the steps.

"You'll see," said Henry feebly. But, he thought, how *am* I going to pull them? To stall for time, he fished through his pockets and found a piece of string. "Uh ... how come you fellows are wearing hats?" he ventured.

"Come on, Robert," said Scooter. "He said he was going to pull his teeth, but I guess he didn't mean it."

" 'Course I'm going to pull them." Henry was determined not to let the boys get away before he found out what had happened. He carefully untangled the string and tried to sound casual. "Did you fellows get your hair cut?" he asked.

"We sure did," said Scooter, "and it's all your fault."

"What do you mean, it's all my fault?" asked Henry. "What did I do?"

"You know." Scooter scowled at Henry. "And if you ask me it was a pretty mean trick. As bad as telling tales."

"Worse," said Robert.

"What mean trick?" Henry demanded. "What are you talking about?"

"Your mother phoned our mothers and told them about the sale of hair clippers, that's what," said Scooter. "She phoned just like you told her to. And they both went straight over to the clipper sale at the Colossal Drugstore."

"My mother?" Henry was genuinely bewildered. "My mother phoned your mothers?"

"Honest, didn't you know about it?" Robert asked.

"Cross my heart and hope to die," said Henry. Well, so that was what his mother had been thinking about at dinner last night! Leave it to her to think of something. Henry wanted to laugh and shout but he didn't dare, not with Scooter glowering at him.

"See?" said Robert to Scooter. "I told you it wasn't his idea for his mother to tell our mothers. I knew Henry wouldn't do a thing like that and you said he would."

Henry looked injured. "You're some friend, thinking I'd do a mean thing like that."

"Well, maybe you didn't," said Scooter grudgingly, "but I bet you haven't really thought of a way to pull your teeth."

"I have, too," said Henry. Now how was he going to get out of his fix, he wondered, as he slowly tied one end of the string to his right tooth. Then he slowly tied the other end of the string to his left tooth while he tried to think of a way to stall for time. "How about letting me have a look at your hair?" he suggested, anxious to see if their haircuts were worse than his.

"Come on! Let's see you pull your teeth," said Scooter.

"I need some more string," explained Henry. "I can't pull them until somebody gives me some more string." Robert and Scooter searched their pockets. "I don't have any," said Robert.

"Me neither," said Scooter. "You're just stalling."

"I'm not stalling." Should he suggest they go around to the back yard, Henry wondered. Maybe he could climb the cherry tree and hang the string that joined his two teeth over a branch and jump out of the tree. It was not much of an idea, but it would have to do.

Henry started to call Ribsy, who was napping with his nose on his paws, when suddenly he had an inspiration. Of course! Why hadn't he thought of it before! All he needed was a little co-operation from Ribsy, and this time he had a feeling that for once Ribsy would do the right thing at the right time.

Henry picked up Ribsy's tug-of-war rope. He tied one end to the middle of the string that joined his two teeth and tossed the other end on to the grass. "Here, Ribsy," he called. Ribsy opened one eye and looked at Henry.

Then he opened the other eye and bounded across the lawn. "Wuf!" he said.

Henry braced himself in case it hurt to have his teeth pulled. Ribsy grabbed the end of the rope, growled deep in his throat, and tugged. Henry's teeth flew out of his mouth so fast he didn't even feel them go.

Henry put his hand to his mouth and stared at his teeth lying on the grass. They had come out so easily he could scarcely believe they were gone. He poked his tongue into the right hole in his mouth and then into the left hole. They were gone, all right. "How's that for a way to pull teeth?" he asked. "They were canine teeth, so I thought I'd let my dog pull them out."

"Say, that was a smart idea," exclaimed Robert. "I never heard of anyone having a dog pull his teeth before. Maybe I can get him to pull the next one I have loose."

"Good old Ribsy," said Henry, and hugged him. Maybe Ribsy did get into a little trouble once in a while, but he was pretty useful for getting out of a tight spot. Ribsy wriggled with delight and licked Henry's face with his long pink tongue.

"A tooth-pulling dog. That's pretty good." Scooter sounded impressed. "Take you long to train the old rubbish hound?"

"Not very long, and he's *not* a rubbish hound." Henry untied his teeth and put them in the watch pocket of his jeans for safekeeping till he put them under his pillow that night. "He's a smart dog, aren't you, Ribsy?"

"Wuf," answered Ribsy, and worried the rope.

Henry looked at Scooter's and Robert's sailor hats. "Well, how about letting me see your haircuts?" he asked, pulling off his own hat.

"Nope." Scooter took hold of his hat and tried to yank it farther down over his ears.

"Aw, come on, Scoot," coaxed Henry. "I pulled my teeth like I said I would."

Robert snatched off his own hat, and he and Henry studied each other's haircuts. "Yours is better at the front but mine is better at the back," Robert decided. "At least it feels better."

Henry examined Robert's hair. It looked pretty bad, a little worse than his own he decided, especially where it was gouged out over the left ear. "I suppose hair really does grow pretty fast," said Henry.

"Anyway, we're better off than Scooter," observed Robert. "He's bald on one side. It'll take months to grow out."

"No kidding?" said Henry. "Really bald?" Then he and Robert began to laugh.

Scooter looked even gloomier. "It's all right for you guys to laugh. You're in the same room at school and you can stick together, but I'll be the only one in my room who has a home-made haircut."

"Gee, that's tough," said Robert, but he didn't sound very sorry.

"It sure is," agreed Henry cheerfully. What did he care about his haircut? As Scooter said, he and Robert could stick together.

Then Henry had an idea. "Hey, fellows, look!" he said. He turned on the garden hose, filled his mouth with water and blew as hard as he could. Two streams of water shot through the gaps in his teeth. "I bet you wish you could spit 'double," he said. Boy, oh, boy! He still had something to show the kids at school. Something besides his haircut.

THE PRETEND PONY

Barbee Oliver Carleton

There once was a boy named Pee-wee who wanted a pony so much that he could think of nothing else. "Come to supper!" his mother would call.

Pee-wee washed his hands and sat down at the table nicely enough. But right away he started thinking about that pony. Soon his supper was stone-cold, and everybody else was finished.

"Bedtime, Pee-wee," his father would say. Pee-wee started off well enough by cleaning his teeth and scrubbing his ears. But sooner or later he began thinking about the pony. There they would find him in the morning, sound asleep on the rug, with his clothes still on and a wishful smile on his face.

"Something has to be done about that pony," said Pee-wee's mother.

"But not this year," said Father.

So they shook their heads and did nothing about the pony at all.

Soon Pee-wee's jolly Uncle Wally came to visit. When he saw that the pony was all Pee-wee could think about, he said, "Pee-wee, you just PRETEND you have that pony. If you pretend a thing hard enough, sometimes it comes true."

Pee-wee grew excited for the first time in weeks. "How long will it take?" he cried.

Jolly Uncle Wally scratched his head. "Oh, I should say maybe three days."

"Now, Wally," said Pee-wee's mother.

But Pee-wee got right to work. First of all, he had to have a pony shed. The old woodshed would do, Pee-wee decided. All that first morning he worked. He cleaned out the shed and swept it carefully. He nailed down planks to mend the floor. He tacked tarred paper on to the roof to keep the pony dry. And all the time he worked, Pee-wee pretended hard that the pony was just outside, grazing in the grass.

When they called him to supper, Pee-wee rode fast across the field on the pretend pony. He reached the house a great deal sooner than ever before.

"How strange!" said Pee-wee's mother, watching at the window. "Pee-wee seems to be several feet off the ground!"

"So he does," said Father, peering. "That boy is pretending that pony so hard, I can almost see it myself!"

Jolly Uncle Wally just puffed on his pipe.

That was the first day.

On the second day, Pee-wee built the pony stall. For the walls, he used some old planks that were out behind the shed. After that, he built a fine feed bin, just as high as a pony's nose. Next he built a shelf to hold the water pail. And all day long, as hard as he worked, Pee-wee pretended even harder. He pretended that his pony was grazing just outside the shed, and that he was brown with maybe a white star on his soft nose.

When they called him to supper, Pee-wee untied the pretend pony. He clucked his tongue and galloped to the house in less time than it takes to tell about it.

Father blinked his eyes. "I must need glasses very badly," he said. "Pee-wee seems to be several feet off the ground again."

"Not only that," whispered Pee-wee's mother. "He appears to be mounted on S O M E T H I N G BROWN!"

Pee-wee tied the pretend pony to the porch rail and came in, not one bit out of breath. Jolly Uncle Wally gave Pee-wee a broad wink, and kept on puffing his pipe.

That was the second day.

On the third and last day, Pee-wee worked hard to put up a fence. All that morning, jolly Uncle Wally helped him. But he had to go away for a while, so Pee-wee finished the fence by himself. Last of all, he filled the pony's water pail and fed him.

But not for a minute did Pee-wee forget to pretend. He pretended that the brown pony with the white star on his nose was just outside, grazing in the field. He even pretended that his brown pony had a golden tan cowboy saddle with a new rope coiled on the pommel. He pretended harder than ever before. He pretended so hard that his hair felt tight around his head.

When they called him to supper, Pee-wee went outside the shed. Sure enough, just as jolly Uncle Wally had said, the pony had come true! He was soft brown, with a white star on his nose, and he wore a golden tan cowboy saddle with a new rope coiled on the pommel. Pee-wee stroked the pony's neck. His coat was soft and his breath was warm and sweet.

Pee-wee's mother and father looked out of the window and their eyes grew very round. "A brown pony with a saddle," Mother whispered. "I never would have believed it!"

Father shook his head. "I still don't," he said.

Jolly Uncle Wally walked across the field, puffing on his pipe. Proudly, Pee-wee rode up to him. "Looks as though I pretended hard enough, doesn't it?" he said.

"Looks that way," smiled Uncle Wally.

DRIBBLE

Judy Blume

I will never forget Friday, May tenth. It's the most important day of my life. It didn't start out that way. It started out ordinary. I went to school. I ate my lunch. I had gym. And then I walked home from school with Jimmy Fargo. We planned to meet at our special rock in the park as soon as we changed our clothes.

In the elevator I told Henry I was glad summer was coming. Henry said he was too. When I got out at my floor I walked down the hall and opened the door to my apartment. I took off my jacket and hung it in the closet. I put my books on the hall table next to my mother's purse. I went straight to my room to change my clothes and check Dribble.

The first thing I noticed was my chain latch. It was unhooked. My bedroom door was open. And there was a chair smack in the middle of my doorway. I nearly tumbled over it. I ran to my dresser to check Dribble. He wasn't there! His bowl with the rocks and water was there – but Dribble was gone.

I got really scared. I thought, *Maybe he died while I was at school and I didn't know about it.* So I rushed into the kitchen and hollered, "Mom ... where's Dribble?" My mother was baking something. My brother sat on the kitchen floor, banging pots and pans together. "Be quite!" I yelled at Fudge. "I can't hear anything with all that noise."

"What did you say, Peter?" my mother asked me.

"I said I can't find Dribble. Where is he?"

"You mean he's not in his bowl?" my mother asked.

I shook my head.

"Oh dear!" my mother said. "I hope he's not crawling around somewhere. You know I don't like the way he smells. I'm going to have a look in the bedrooms. You check in here, Peter."

My mother hurried off. I looked at my brother. He was smiling. "Fudge, do you know where Dribble is?" I asked calmly.

Fudge kept smiling.

"Did you take him? Did you, Fudge?" I asked, not so calmly.

Fudge giggled and covered his mouth with his hands.

I yelled. "Where is he? What did you do with my turtle?"

No answer from Fudge. He banged his pots and pans together again. I yanked the pots out of his hand. I tried to speak softly. "Now tell me where Dribble is. Just tell me where my turtle is. I won't be mad if you tell me. Come on, Fudge ... please."

Fudge looked up at me. "In tummy," he said.

"What do you mean, in tummy?" I asked, narrowing my eyes.

"Dribble in tummy!" he repeated.

"What tummy!" I shouted at my brother.

"This one," Fudge said, rubbing his stomach. "Dribble in this tummy! Right here!"

I decided to go along with his game. "Okay. How did he get in there, Fudge?" I asked.

Fudge stood up. He jumped up and down and sang out, "I ATE HIM ... ATE HIM ... ATE HIM!" Then he ran out of the room.

My mother came back into the kitchen. "Well, I just can't find him anywhere," she said. "I looked in all the dresser drawers and the bathroom cabinets and the shower and the tub and ..."

"Mom," I said, shaking my head. "How could you?"

"How could I what, Peter?" Mom asked.

"How could you let him do it?"

"Let who do what, Peter?" Mom asked.

"LET FUDGE EAT DRIBBLE!" I screamed.

My mother started to mix whatever she was baking. "Don't be silly, Peter," she said. "Dribble is a turtle."

"HE ATE DRIBBLE!" I insisted.

"*Peter Warren Hatcher!* STOP SAYING THAT!" Mom hollered.

"Well, ask him. Go ahead and ask him," I told her.

Fudge was standing in the kitchen doorway with a big grin on his face. My mother picked him up and patted his head. "Fudgie," she said to him, "tell Mommy where brother's turtle is."

"In tummy," Fudge said.

"What tummy?" Mom asked.

"Mine!" Fudge laughed.

My mother put Fudge down on the kitchen counter where he couldn't get away from her. "Oh, you're fooling Mommy ... right?"

"No fool!" Fudge said.

My mother turned very pale. "You really ate your brother's turtle?"

Big smile from Fudge.

"You mean that you put him in your mouth and chewed him up ... like this?" Mom made believe she was chewing.

"No," Fudge said.

A smile of relief crossed my mother's face. "Of course you didn't. It's just a joke." She put Fudge down on the floor and gave me a *look*.

Fudge babbled. "No chew, no chew. Gulp... gulp... all gone turtle. Down Fudge's tummy."

Me and my mother stared at Fudge.

"You didn't!" Mom said.

"Did so!" Fudge said.

"No!" Mom shouted.

"Yes!" Fudge shouted back.

"Yes?" Mom asked weakly, holding onto a chair with both hands.

"Yes!" Fudge beamed.

My mother moaned and picked up my brother. "Oh no! My angel! My precious little baby! OH ... NO..."

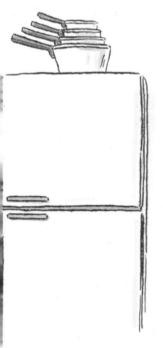

My mother didn't stop to think about my turtle. She didn't even give Dribble a thought. She didn't even stop to wonder how my turtle liked being swallowed by my brother. She ran to the phone with Fudge tucked under one arm. I followed. Mom dialled the operator and cried, "Oh help! This is an emergency. My baby ate a turtle ... STOP THAT LAUGHING," my mother told the operator. "Send an ambulance right away; 25 West 68th Street."

Mom hung up. She didn't look too well. Tears were running down her face. She put Fudge down on the floor. I couldn't understand why she was so upset. Fudge seemed just fine.

"Help me, Peter," Mom begged. "Get me blankets."

I ran into my brother's room. I grabbed two blankets from Fudge's bed. He was following me around with that silly grin on his face. I felt like giving him a pinch. How could he stand there looking so happy when he had my turtle inside him?

I delivered the blankets to my mother. She wrapped Fudge up in them and ran to the front door. I followed and grabbed her purse from the hall table. I figured she'd be glad I thought of that.

Out in the hall I pressed the elevator buzzer. We had to wait a few minutes. Mom paced up and down in front of the elevator. Fudge was cradled in her arms. He sucked his fingers and made that slurping noise I like. But all I could think of was Dribble.

Finally, the elevator got to our floor. There were three people in it besides Henry. "This is an emergency," Mom wailed. "The ambulance is waiting downstairs. Please hurry!"

"Yes, Mrs Hatcher. Of course," Henry said. "I'll run her down just as fast as I can. No other stops."

Someone poked me in the back. I turned

around. It was Mrs Rudder. "What's the matter?" she whispered.

"It's my brother," I whispered back. "He ate my turtle."

Mrs Rudder whispered *that* to the man next to her and *he* whispered it to the lady next to *him* who whispered it to Henry. I faced front and pretended I didn't hear anything.

My mother turned around with Fudge in her arms and said, "That's not funny. Not funny at all!"

But Fudge said, "Funny, funny, funny Fudge!"

Everybody laughed. Everybody except my mother.

The elevator door opened. Two men, dressed in white, were waiting with a stretcher. "This the baby?" one of them asked.

"Yes. Yes, it is," Mom sobbed.

"Don't worry, lady. We'll be to the hospital in no time."

"Come, Peter," my mother said, tugging at my sleeve. "We're going to ride in the ambulance with Fudge."

My mother and I climbed into the back of the blue ambulance. I was never in one before. It was neat. Fudge kneeled on a cot and peered out through the window. He waved at the crowd of people that had gathered on the sidewalk.

One of the attendants sat in the back with us. The other one was driving. "What seems to be the trouble, lady?" the attendant asked. "This kid looks pretty healthy to me."

"He swallowed a turtle," my mother whispered.

"He did WHAT?" the attendant asked.

"Ate my turtle. That's what!" I told him.

My mother covered her face with her hanky and started to cry again.

"Hey, Joe!" the attendant called to the driver. "Make it snappy ... *this* one swallowed a turtle!"

"That's not funny!" Mom insisted. I didn't think so either, considering it was my turtle!

We arrived at the back door of the hospital. Fudge was whisked away by two nurses. My mother ran after him. "You wait here, young man," another nurse called to me, pointing to a bench.

41

I sat down on the hard, wooden bench. I didn't have anything to do. There weren't any books or magazines spread out, like when I go to Dr Cone's office. So I watched the clock and read all the signs on the walls. I found out I was in the emergency section of the hospital.

After a while the nurse came back. She gave me some paper and crayons. "Here you are. Be a good boy and draw some pictures. Your mother will be out soon."

I wondered if she knew about Dribble and that's why she was trying to be nice to me. I didn't feel like drawing any pictures. I wondered what they were doing to Fudge in there. Maybe he wasn't such a bad little guy after all. I remembered that Jimmy Fargo's little cousin once swallowed the most valuable rock from Jimmy's collection. And my mother told me that when I was a little kid I swallowed a quarter. Still . . . a quarter's not like a turtle!

I watched the clock on the wall for an hour and ten minutes. Then a door opened and my mother stepped out with Dr Cone. I was surprised to see him. I didn't know he worked in the hospital.

"Hello, Peter," he said.

"Hello, Dr Cone. Did you get my turtle?"

"Not yet, Peter," he said. "But I do have something to show you. Here are some X-rays of your brother."

I studied the X-rays as Dr Cone
pointed things out to me.

"You see," he said.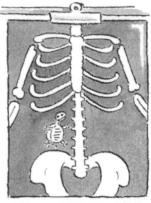
"There's your turtle . . .
right there."

I looked hard. "Will
Dribble be in there for
ever?" I asked.

"No. Definitely not!
We'll get him out. We
gave Fudge some medicine
already. That should do the
trick nicely."

"What kind of medicine?" I asked. "What
trick?"

"Castor oil, Peter," my mother said. "Fudge
took castor oil. And milk of magnesia. And prune
juice too. Lots of that. All those things will help to
get Dribble out of Fudge's tummy."

"We just have to wait," Dr Cone said. "Probably
until tomorrow or the day after. Fudge will have to
spend the night here. But I don't think he's going
to be swallowing anything that he isn't supposed to
be swallowing from now on."

"How about Dribble?" I asked. "Will Dribble
be all right?" My mother and Dr Cone looked at
each other. I knew the answer before he shook his
head and said, "I think you may have to get a new
turtle, Peter."

"I don't want a new turtle!" I said. Tears came to my eyes. I was embarrassed and wiped them away with the back of my hand. Then my nose started to run and I had to sniffle. "I want Dribble," I said. "That's the only turtle I want."

My mother took me home in a taxi. She told me my father was on his way to the hospital to be with Fudge. When we got home she made me lamb chops for dinner, but I wasn't very hungry. My father came home late that night. I was still up. My father looked gloomy. He whispered to my mother, "Not yet ... nothing yet."

The next day was Saturday. No school. I spent the whole day in the hospital waiting room. There were plenty of people around. And magazines and books too. It wasn't like the hard bench in the emergency hallway. It was more like a living-room. I told everybody that my brother ate my turtle. They looked at me kind of funny. But nobody ever said they were sorry to hear about my turtle. Not once.

My mother joined me for supper in the hospital coffee shop. I ordered a hamburger but I left most of it, because right in the middle of supper my mother told me that if the medicine didn't work soon Fudge might have to have an operation to get Dribble out of him. My mother didn't eat anything.

That night my grandmother came to stay with me. My mother and father stayed at the hospital with Fudge. Things were pretty dreary at home. Every hour the phone rang. It was my mother calling from the hospital with a report.

"Not yet . . . I see," Grandma repeated. "Nothing happening yet."

I was miserable. I was lonely. Grandma didn't notice. I even missed Fudge banging his pots and pans together. In the middle of the night the phone rang again. It woke me up and I crept out into the hallway to hear what was going on.

Grandma shouted, "Whoopee! It's out! Good news at last."

She hung up and turned to me. "The medicine has finally worked, Peter. All that castor oil and milk of magnesia and prune juice finally worked. The turtle is out!"

"Alive or dead?" I asked.

"PETER WARREN HATCHER, WHAT A QUESTION!" Grandma shouted.

So my brother no longer had a turtle inside of him. And I no longer had a turtle! I didn't like Fudge as much as I thought I did before the phone rang.

The next morning Fudge came home from the hospital. My father carried him into the apartment. My mother's arms were loaded with presents. All for Fudge! My mother put the presents down and kissed him. She said, "Fudgie can have anything he wants. Anything at all. Mommy's so happy her baby's all better!"

It was disgusting. Presents and kisses and attention for Fudge. I couldn't even look at him. He was having fun! He probably wasn't even sorry he ate my turtle.

That night my father came home with the biggest box of all. It wasn't wrapped up or anything but I knew it was another present. I turned away from my father.

"Peter," he said. "This box is a surprise for you!"

"Well, I don't want another turtle" I said. "Don't think you can make me feel better with another turtle...because you can't."

"Who said anything about a turtle, son?" Dad asked.

"You see, Peter, your mother and I think you've been a good sport about the whole situation. After all, Dribble *was* your pet."

I looked up. Could I be hearing right? Did they

really remember about me and Dribble? I put my hand inside the box. I felt something warm and soft and furry. I knew it was a dog, but I pretended to be surprised when he jumped up on my lap and licked me.

Fudge cried, "Ohhh ... doggie! See ... doggie!" He ran right over and grabbed my dog's tail.

"Fudge," my father said, taking him away. "This is your brother's dog. Maybe someday you'll have a dog of your own. But this one belongs to Peter. Do you understand?"

Fudge nodded. "Pee-tah's dog."

"That's right," my father said. "Peter's dog!" Then he turned to me. "And just to be sure, son," he said, "We got a dog that's going to grow quite big. *Much* too big for your brother to swallow!"

We all laughed. My dog was neat.

I named him Turtle ... to remind me.

A PET
FIT FOR A KING

Liss Norton

King Kevin wanted a pet. Not a dog or cat. Not even a budgie or a goldfish. He wanted an *unusual* pet. A pet fit for a king. He phoned the pet shop. "Please send me a special pet," he said.

"We've got a South American glitter snake, Your Majesty," the pet shop lady said. "I'm sure you'd like it."

"Please send it along to the castle," said King Kevin.

The South American glitter snake was beautiful. Its gold and silver scales glittered in the sunlight. "Perfect," King Kevin said as he took it out of the box. "This is a pet fit for a king." He stroked the snake's back and it hissed happily.

The snake was great fun. It played a game that King Kevin called hide and shriek. It hid in a cup- board and made Simmons the butler nearly jump out of his skin. It hid in the long grass and made Old Peg the gardener jump so high she landed in a tree. It hid in the kitchen and made Mrs Bakewell drop the cabbage she'd cooked for dinner. King Kevin was very glad about that. He hated cabbage.

Bedtime came. King Kevin changed into his pyjamas and cleaned his teeth. He searched for the glitter snake but he couldn't find it. "It must be hiding," he said with a grin. "I expect it wants to frighten somebody." He went into his bedroom. He pulled back the bedclothes. The glitter snake sprang up with a loud hiss. "Aaagh!" screamed King Kevin. He fell over backwards BUMP! and bruised his bottom.

The next morning King Kevin took the glitter snake back to the pet shop. "It wasn't quite right for me," he said, "I'd like a parrot instead."

The parrot was beautiful. It had red, green, blue and yellow feathers. It had bright eyes and a curved beak. "*This* is a pet fit for a king," King Kevin said happily. The parrot flew on to his shoulder and King Kevin carried it back to the castle.

The soldiers were practising their marching in the courtyard. "Quick march!" Captain Gruff commanded.

"Quick march," squawked the parrot.

King Kevin was delighted. He'd forgotten that parrots can talk.

"Right wheel," cried the Captain.

"Right wheel," echoed the parrot.

King Kevin stroked the parrot's feathery chest. "I knew you'd be a good pet," he said.

"I knew you'd be a good pet," screeched the parrot.

They watched the soldiers for a long time and the parrot learnt to repeat every order he heard. At last Captain Gruff marched off to have a cup of tea. He left the soldiers standing smartly to attention.

"Quick march," the parrot squawked. The soldiers began to march. "Right wheel," shrieked the parrot. The soldiers turned right. Some of them bumped into the castle wall and had to sit down.

"About turn," screeched the parrot. "At the

double." The soldiers turned round so quickly they got their swords tangled together. King Kevin laughed and laughed.

Captain Gruff heard the commotion. He ran into the courtyard. "What's going on?" he bellowed. He looked so angry that King Kevin ran away. The parrot held on tightly to his shoulder.

They hid behind the bathroom door. "The Captain will never find us here," said King Kevin.

"The Captain will never find us here," squawked the parrot.

King Kevin heard heavy footsteps clumping up the stairs. "Shhh," he hissed.

"Shhh," said the parrot.

"Don't say another word or he'll hear us," King Kevin whispered.

"Don't say another word or he'll hear us," screeched the parrot.

The footsteps stamped along the passage. They halted outside the bathroom door. "Where are you, Your Majesty?" Captain Gruff said crossly.

"Where are you, Your Majesty?" echoed the parrot.

King Kevin glared at the parrot. He didn't want a pet that gave away his hiding places. He came out of the bathroom. Captain Gruff looked furious. No more parrots for me, King Kevin thought.

The pet shop lady was surprised to see King Kevin and the parrot. "What's wrong with him, Your Majesty?" she asked.

"He talks too much," King Kevin said.

The pet shop lady nodded. "Which pet would you like now?"

King Kevin explored the shop. There were so many different pets to choose from. He liked the scaly crocodile with the sharp white teeth. He liked the lizard that changed colour. He liked the huge hippo that yawned when he tickled its tummy. He liked the upside-down bat. He especially liked the fluffy black tarantula. But he knew they would all cause trouble at the castle.

At last he spotted a tiny brown monkey. He bent down for a closer look. The monkey sprang up.

It stretched out a little paw. It held King Kevin's finger. "I'll have this monkey," King Kevin said. "And I'll call him Marmaduke."

On the way back to the castle, Marmaduke curled up in King Kevin's arms like a baby. King Kevin stroked the monkey's soft fur. "No one can complain about *you*," he said.

But he was wrong.

Marmaduke liked living in the castle. He snatched the feather duster from Polly the chambermaid. He turned somersaults in the courtyard and made the soldiers laugh so much they forgot to guard  the castle. He stole bananas from the kitchen and left the skins where Simmons the butler was sure to slip on them. He even dug up one of Old Peg's prize rose bushes.

Everyone in the castle came to see King Kevin. "That monkey has got to go, Your Majesty," they cried. "We can't do our jobs with him around."

King Kevin stroked Marmaduke's head. He really loved the little monkey and he didn't want to send him back to the pet shop. But he was the king and kings have to set a good example. "All right," King Kevin said sadly. He wiped away a tear. "I'll take him back to the pet shop in the morning."

Morning came. Sadly King Kevin picked up the little monkey. He didn't want to take Marmaduke back to the pet shop but he knew he had to. He carried the monkey outside. A strong wind had sprung up during the night. Marmaduke shivered in King Kevin's arms. "Don't worry," King Kevin said. "You'll be quite safe with me. I won't let you blow away." As he spoke there was an extra-strong gust of wind. King Kevin's crown flew off his head. It whirled up into the air.

"Help!" King Kevin cried. "My crown's blown away."

Captain Gruff and the soldiers ran out into the courtyard. The wind lifted the crown high above the roofs of the castle. "The royal crown has blown away," Captain Gruff bellowed.

Mrs Bakewell the cook ran out of the kitchen. She was holding a bowl full of chocolate pudding mix and a wooden spoon. "The royal crown has blown away," she cried.

Old Peg ran up from the garden. "The royal crown has blown away," she said.

Simmons the butler and Polly and the chambermaid peered out of an upstairs window. "The royal crown has blown away," they gasped.

Suddenly the wind dropped. The crown began to fall. It spun round and round, falling faster and faster. It landed on top of the highest tower in the castle. "Oh no!" everyone cried. "We'll never get it down from there." King Kevin knew they were right. The longest ladder in the kingdom wouldn't reach to the top of that tower.

Suddenly Marmaduke sprang out of King Kevin's arms. He ran across the courtyard and began to climb. He clambered up the castle walls. He clung to the stones. "Be careful," King Kevin cried.

The monkey reached the battlements. He clambered over. He climbed up the side of a tower. Soon he was scrambling up the roof of the highest tower in the castle. At last he reached the top. He picked up the crown and started to climb down again. "He's done it!" Polly cried.

It didn't take Marmaduke long to reach the ground. He ran across to King Kevin. He climbed up King Kevin's back and plonked the crown on his head. "The royal crown is safe!" everyone cried. "Marmaduke is a hero. Three cheers for Marmaduke."

King Kevin stroked the little monkey's head. "Does this mean I can keep Marmaduke?" he asked hopefully.

"Keep Marmaduke? of course you can, Your Majesty," everyone said. "He's a pet fit for a king!"

RESCUING
THE RESCUERS

Malorie Blackman

"I want a dog," I said.

"I want a cat," said Antony.

"I want a rabbit," said Edward.

Mum put her hands on her hips. "I'm not getting three different pets. In fact I'm not sure I should even get one."

"But ..." I said.

"But ..." said Antony.

"But ..." Edward repeated.

"No buts!" Mum argued. "I don't think you three realize how much work is involved in owning a pet."

"We do!" I said.

"We do!" said Antony.

"We do!" Edward repeated.

Then Mum got a funny look in her eyes. The same look she gets when she has one of her ideas and she thinks it's a good one. I wonder why her ideas always seem to get me and the twins into trouble?

"Stay there you three. I'll be right back," Mum said, and off she dashed.

My brothers and I looked at each other and shrugged. Before we got bored just standing and waiting, Mum came back with a large box in her hands.

"What's in the box?" we asked.

Mum put the box down on the carpet. We peered into it.

"A cat!" I said, surprised.

"It's Mr McBain's cat. Her name is Syrup because she's the exact same colour as golden syrup."

Mr McBain is our other next-door neighbour. He's a tall, elderly man with hair that only grows on the sides of his head. The top of his head is shiny and smooth like an egg.

"How come we've got her?" Antony asked.

"Yeah! How come?" asked Edward.

"If you three can look after Syrup for this week-end without getting into trouble then we'll talk seriously about which pet to get – but only then," Mum said.

"What do we do first?" I asked.

Antony, Edward and I knelt down around the box.

"First, take Syrup out of the box. Then take her litter tray out of the box and put it in the conservatory near the washing machine. Then you can feed her. Mr McBain also gave me two tins of cat food. They're in my trouser pockets. After that you can play with her," Mum said.

So I picked Syrup out of the box and held her against my chest and stroked her. She was warm and her fur was soft. Her breath tickled my face. I liked her.

"Maybe we should have a cat and not a dog," I thought.

Antony took out Syrup's litter tray and put it in the conservatory. Edward got the two tins of cat food out of Mum's tracksuit trouser pockets.

"Later on we'll all have to pop to the shop at the top of the road and get some more cat food," said Mum.

Mum opened one of the tins and put the food in Syrup's bowl which was also in the box. We all crouched down around Syrup as she ate.

"I want a cat, Mum," I said.

"So do I," Antony said.

"Yeah! Me too!" said Edward.

"We'll see," was all Mum said.

After Syrup had eaten her lunch we took her outside whilst Mum went to watch the telly. I was still holding her.

"Syrup, this is our garden," I said.

"Miaow!" Syrup replied,
having a look around.

Then, before any of us had a chance to blink,
Syrup struggled out of my arms, scurried across
our garden and scooted up our apple tree.

"What do we do now?" Antony asked.

"Yeah! What?" asked Edward.

"We can't call Mum," I said. "She'll say we can't
look after a pet for one minute without getting
into trouble."

"So what *are* we going to do?" asked Antony.

"Yeah! What?" Edward repeated.

So I said, "This is a job for Girl Wonder and . . ."

"The Terrific Twins!" Antony and Edward
grinned.

Then we all spun around until we were dizzy.

"All right, Terrific Twins, I have a plan," I said.
"We'll climb up the tree and get Syrup
down."

And that's what we did. Slowly
and carefully, we each climbed

60

up the tree. (I helped the twins get onto the first branch as they couldn't quite reach it.) Up and up we went. Up and up. And above us I could see Syrup staring down at us.

Just as we got close to her, guess what she did?

She yawned. She stretched her back. Then she scooted *down* the tree.

"Huh! Why didn't she do that *before* we came up here?" I said.

We all looked down. The ground looked far, *far* away.

"What are you kids up to?" Mr McBain called out from his garden.

"What do you children think you're doing?" shouted Miss Ree from her garden. "Get down at once before you hurt yourselves."

I looked at Antony and Edward and they looked at me. Then we all burst into tears.

"We can't get down," I sobbed. "The ground is far, *far* away."

Then Mum came running out into the garden.

"Maxine, Antony, Edward, what have you been doing now?" she said, her hands on her hips.

"We were trying to rescue the cat," I sniffed.

"Maxine, cats climb up trees all the time. Unlike you lot, they have no trouble climbing down either. You should have left Syrup up there," Mr McBain said.

"Mum, I want to come down," wailed Antony.

"Yeah! Me too!" Edward joined in.

"I'm going to have to call the Fire Brigade," Mum said.

Within minutes we heard the sound of the fire engine siren – DRING DRING DRING DRING! Mum ran into the house to let them in. Seconds later she came out into the garden followed by a firewoman and three firemen. They all stood below our apple tree. We peered down at them. We'd never seen firepeople up close before. The firemen placed two ladders against the trunk of the tree.

"It's all right. We'll soon have you down," said the firewoman.

"Don't worry," said one of the firemen. "You'll soon be on the ground."

They carried Antony and Edward down first. I looked around. I could see across all the neighbours' gardens. *Everyone* was watching us.

"All right, Maxine, take my hands," said the firewoman, lifting me round onto her back. "I'm going to give you a piggyback ride. In Scotland we call it a collybucky."

"A collybucky! That's a funny name." I laughed.

"No funnier than piggyback," said the firewoman. "Here we are down on the ground."

I looked around, surprised. I hadn't even noticed us coming down.

"Say thank you to the firepeople," Mum said.

"Thank you very much," we said.

"Right, you three – go into the house. I've got a few things to say to you," Mum said sternly. "And Syrup is going straight back to Mr McBain."

We went into the kitchen and looked through the window. Mum was talking to the firepeople.

"Mum's going to spend forever telling us off now," Antony said to me, annoyed.

"Yeah! Forever!" Edward agreed.

"Your plan was stinky," Antony grumbled.

"Yeah! Seriously stinky," Edward mumbled.

"But it worked, didn't it?" I said. "We *did* get Syrup out of the tree."

ARABEL'S RAVEN

Joan Aiken

On a stormy night in March, not long ago, a respectable taxi-driver named Ebenezer Jones found himself driving home, very late, through the somewhat wild and sinister district of London known as Rumbury Town. Mr Jones was passing the long, desolate piece of land called Rumbury Waste, when, in the street not far ahead, he observed a large, dark, upright object. It was rather smaller than a coalhod, but bigger than a quart cider-bottle, and it was moving slowly from one side of the street to the other.

· Mr Jones had approached to within about twenty yards of this object when a motor-cyclist, with a pillion passenger, shot by him at a reckless pace and cut in very close. Mr Jones braked sharply, looking in his rear-view mirror. When he looked forward again he saw that the motor-cycle must have struck the upright object in passing, for it was now lying on its side, just ahead of his front wheels.

He brought his taxi to a halt. "Not but what I daresay I'm being foolish," he thought. "There's plenty in this part of town that's best left alone. But you can't see something like that happen without stopping to have a look."

He got out of his cab.

What he found in the road was a large black bird, almost two feet long, with a hairy fringe round its beak. At first he thought it was dead. But as he got nearer, it opened one eye slightly, then shut it again.

"Poor thing; it's probably stunned," thought Mr Jones.

His horoscope in the *Hackney Drivers' Herald* that morning had said, "Due to your skill, a life will be saved today." Mr Jones had been worrying as he drove home, because up till now he had not, so far as he knew, saved any lives that day, except by avoiding pedestrians recklessly crossing the road without looking.

"This'll be the life I'm due to save," he thought. "Must be, for it's five to midnight now," and he went back to his cab for the bottle of brandy and teaspoon he always carried in the tool-kit in case lady passengers turned faint.

It is not at all easy to give brandy to a large bird lying unconscious in the road. After five minutes there was a good deal of brandy on the cobbles, and some up Mr Jones's sleeve, and some in his shoes, but he could not be sure that any had actually gone down the bird's throat. The difficulty was that he needed at least three hands: one to hold the bottle, one to hold the spoon, and one to hold the bird's beak open. If he prised open the beak with the handle of the teaspoon, it was sure to shut again before he had time to reverse the spoon and tip in some brandy.

Suddenly a hand fell on Mr Jones's shoulder.

"Just what do you think you're doing?" inquired one of two policemen who had left their van and were standing over him.

The other sniffed in a disapproving manner. Mr Jones straightened slowly.

"I was just giving some brandy to this rook," he explained. He was rather embarrassed, because he had spilt such a lot of the brandy.

"Rook? That's no rook," said the officer who had sniffed. "That's a raven. Look at its hairy beak."

"Whatever it is, it's stunned," said Mr Jones. "A motorbike hit it."

"Ah," said the second officer, "that'll have been one of the pair who just pinched thirty thousand quid from the bank in the High Street. It's the Cash-and-Carat boys – the ones who've done a lot of burglaries round here lately. Did you see which way they went?"

"No," said Mr Jones, tipping up the raven's head, "but they'll have a dent on their bike. Could one of you hold the bottle for me?"

"You don't want to give him brandy. Hot sweet tea's what you want to give him."

"That's right," said the other policeman. "And an ice-pack under the back of his neck."

"Burn feathers in front of his beak."

"Slap his hands."

"Undo his shoelaces."

"Put him in the fridge."

"He hasn't got any shoelaces," said Mr Jones, not best pleased at all this advice. "If you aren't going to hold the bottle, why don't you go on and catch the blokes that knocked him over?"

"Oh *they'll* be well away by now. Besides, they carry guns. We'll go back to the station," said the first policeman.

"And you'd better not stay here, giving intoxicating liquor to a bird, or we might have to take you in for loitering in a suspicious manner."

"I can't just leave the bird here in the road," said Mr Jones.

"Take it with you, then."

"Can't you take it to the station?"

"Not likely," said the second policeman. "No facilities for ravens there."

They stood with folded arms, watching, while Mr Jones slowly picked up the bird and put it in his taxi. And they were still watching as he started up and drove off.

So that was how Mr Jones happened to take the raven back with him to Number Six, Rainwater Crescent, N.W.3½, on a windy March night.

When he got home, nobody was up, which was not surprising, since it was after midnight. He would have liked to wake his daughter Arabel, who was fond of all birds and animals. But since she was quite young — she hadn't started school yet — he thought he had better not. And he knew he must not wake his wife Martha, because she had to be at work at Round & Round, the gramophone shop in the High Street, at nine in the morning.

He laid the raven on the kitchen floor, opened the window to give it air, put on the kettle for hot sweet tea, and, while he had the match lit, burned a feather-duster under the raven's beak. Nothing happened, except that the smoke made Mr Jones cough. He saw no way of slapping the raven's hands or undoing its shoelaces, so he took some ice-cubes and a jug of milk from the fridge. He left the fridge door open because his hands were full, and anyway it usually swung shut by itself. With great care he slid a little row of ice-cubes under the back of the raven's neck.

The kettle boiled and he made the tea: a spoonful for each person and one for the pot, three in all. He also spread himself a slice of bread and fishpaste because he didn't see why he shouldn't have a little something as well as the bird. He poured out a cup of tea for himself and an egg-cupful for the raven, putting plenty of sugar in both.

But when he turned round, egg-cup in hand, the raven had gone.

"Bless me," Mr Jones said, "there's ingratitude for you! After all my trouble! I suppose he flew out of the window; those ice-cubes certainly did the trick quick. I wonder if it would be a good notion to carry some ice-cubes with me in the cab? I could put them in a vacuum flask – might be better than brandy if lady passengers turn faint . . ."

Thinking these thoughts he finished his tea (and the raven's; no sense in leaving it to get cold), turned out the light, and went to bed.

In the middle of the night he thought, "Did I put the milk back in the fridge?"

And he thought, "No I didn't."

And he thought, "I ought to get up and put it away."

And then he thought, "It's a cold night, the milk's not going to turn between now and breakfast. Besides, Thursday tomorrow, it's my early day."

So he rolled over and went to sleep.

Every Thursday Mr Jones drove the local

fishmonger, Mr Finney, over to Colchester to buy oysters at five in the morning. So, early next day, up he got, off he went. Made himself a cup of tea, finished the milk in the jug, never looked in the fridge.

An hour after he had gone Mrs Jones got up and put on the kettle. Finding the milk jug empty she went yawning to the fridge and pulled the door open, not noticing that it had been prevented from shutting properly by the handle of a burnt featherduster which had fallen against the hinge. But she noticed what was inside the fridge all right. She let out a shriek that brought Arabel running downstairs.

Arabel was little and fair with grey eyes. She was wearing a white nightdress that made her look like a lampshade with two feet sticking out from the bottom. One of the feet had a blue sock on.

71

"What's the matter, Ma?" she said.

"There's a great awful *bird* in the fridge!" sobbed Mrs Jones. "And it's eaten all the cheese and a blackcurrant tart and five pints of milk and a bowl of dripping and a pound of sausages. All that's left is the lettuce."

"Then we'll have lettuce for breakfast," said Arabel.

But Mrs Jones said she didn't fancy lettuce that had spent the night in the fridge with a great awful bird. "And how are we going to get it out of there?"

"The lettuce?"

"The *bird*!" said Mrs Jones, switching off the kettle and pouring hot water into a pot without any tea in it.

Arabel opened the fridge door, which had swung shut. There sat the bird, among the empty milk bottles, but he was a lot bigger than they were. There was a certain amount of wreckage around him – torn foil, and cheese wrappings, and milk splashes, and bits of pastry, and crumbs of dripping, and rejected lettuce leaves. It was like Rumbury Waste after a picnic Sunday.

Arabel looked at the raven, and he looked back at her.

"His name's Mortimer," she said.

"No it's not, no it's not!" cried Mrs Jones, taking a loaf from the bread bin and absent-mindedly

running the tap over it. "We said you could have a hamster when you were five, or a puppy or a kitten when you were six, and of course call it what you wish, oh my *stars*, look at that creature's toe-nails, if nails they can be called, but not a bird like that, a great hairy awful thing eating us out of house and home, as big as a fire extinguisher and all black –" But Arabel was looking at the raven and he was looking back at her.

"His name's Mortimer," she said. And she put both arms round the raven, not an easy thing to do, all jammed in among the milk bottles as he was, and lifted him out.

"He's very heavy," she said, and set him down on the kitchen floor.

"So I should think, considering he's got a pound of sausages, a bowl of dripping, five pints of milk, half a pound of New Zealand cheddar, and a black-currant tart inside him," said Mrs Jones. "I'll open the window. Perhaps he'll fly out."

She opened the window. But Mortimer did not fly out. He was busy examining everything in the kitchen very thoroughly. He tapped the table legs with his beak – they were metal, and clinked. Then he took everything out of the waste bin – a pound of peanut shells, two empty tins, and some jam tart cases. He particularly liked the jam tart cases, which he pushed under the lino. Then he walked over to the fireplace – it was an old-fashioned kitchen –

and began chipping out the mortar from between the bricks.

Mrs Jones had been gazing at the raven as if she were under a spell, but when he began on the fire-place, she said, "*Don't* let him do that!"

"Mortimer," said Arabel, "we'd like you not to do that, please."

Mortimer turned his head right round on its black feathery neck and gave Arabel a thoughtful, considering look. Then he made his first remark, which was a deep, hoarse, rasping croak.

HEAVEN

David Henry Wilson

The gerbils were dead. Daddy had bought them on the twins' first birthday, and so Jeremy James had christened them Wiffer and Jeffer. He'd loved to hold them, and to watch them chasing round their cage, burrowing in the sawdust, or treadling their wheel. But last night they had both been lying quietly, and this morning they were lying dead.

"What made them die?" asked Jeremy James through his tears.

"Difficult to say without a post-mortem," answered Daddy.

"Will the postman bring one?" asked Jeremy James.

"A post-mortem's an examination," said Daddy, "to find the cause of death."

Jeremy James didn't want to examine Wiffer and

Jeffer. He didn't even want to look at them lying there so still and stiff in the corner of their cage.

There had been a death in the family before. Great-Great-Aunt Maud had died at the age of ninety-two, and Jeremy James had gone to her funeral. She had been put in a beautiful shiny box, which Jeremy James would have liked to keep his toys and sweets in. Only the grown-ups had wasted it by putting it in the ground and covering it up with earth.

"We'll just bury them, shall we?" said Daddy. "Somewhere nice in the garden."

"Will we put them in a box?" asked Jeremy James. "Like Great-Great-Aunt Maud?"

"Yes," said Daddy. "Maybe you can go and find one, while I get things ready."

Jeremy James remembered something else about Great-Great-Aunt Maud.

"Can we have a party afterwards as well?" he asked.

"I expect Mummy will let us have a few sandwiches and cakes," said Daddy.

It so happened that Mummy had already planned to make sandwiches and cakes, because the Reverend Cole was coming round to discuss the church fete.

"Maybe if you ask him nicely," said Mummy, "the Reverend Cole might give the gerbils a proper burial."

Jeremy James thought that was a good idea, and so off he went to look for a box, while Mummy made the sandwiches and cakes, and Daddy went out into the garden to dig a grave.

The box that Jeremy James chose was bright and cheerful. Great-Great-Aunt Maud had been buried in one that was heavy and shiny and dark, but she'd been very old, and so maybe she hadn't liked cheerful boxes. The gerbils would have one that was covered in different-coloured blobs, each of which was a pleasure to look at whether you were alive or dead. It was an empty liquorice allsort box.

The Reverend Cole was very old, too, though not as old or as dead as Great-Great-Aunt Maud. He walked with a hobble, and talked with a wobble, and he had accidentally dropped Christopher in the font during the twins' christening. Jeremy

James remembered that day very well, because he had accidentally been the cause of the Reverend Cole accidentally dropping Christopher.

"Never heard of dead marbles," said the Reverend Cole.

"Not marbles," said Jeremy James. "Gerbils."

"Ah!" said the Reverend Cole. "Where are they, then?"

"Here," said Jeremy James, holding out the liquorice allsort box.

"Thank you," said the Reverend Cole. "My favourite sweets."

He took the box, opened the lid, and found himself looking at Wiffer and Jeffer.

"Aaaugh!" he cried, and promptly dropped the box on the floor. Wiffer and Jeffer fell out on to the carpet, while the Reverend Cole did a sort of hobble-jump backwards, bumped straight into the coffee table, and knocked off the teapot that Mummy had just put there.

"Aaaugh!" cried the Reverend Cole again, as hot tea splashed over his leg and foot. Then he hobble-hopped to an armchair, and hobble-slumped into it.

"Oh dear!" said Mummy. "I'm ever so sorry."

She fetched a couple of cloths, and while she wiped the Reverend Cole's shoe and trouser-leg, Daddy mopped up the tea from the carpet. Meanwhile, Wiffer and Jeffer lay next to the liquorice allsort box, and Jeremy James stood

looking at them, with tears dropping out of his eyes.

Eventually, Daddy put them back in their box, Mummy made some more tea, and the Reverend Cole patted Jeremy James on the head.

"No harm done," he said. "Just a drop o' spilt tea. No need to cry."

Jeremy James hadn't been crying because of the spilt tea, but with Wiffer and Jeffer safely back in their box, he stopped crying, and the Reverend Cole congratulated himself on his handling of the situation.

Daddy had dug a little grave under the apple tree, and very solemnly everyone trooped out into the garden. Mummy was holding Christopher, Daddy was holding Jennifer, Jeremy James was holding the box, and the Reverend Cole held forth:

"O Death," he said, "where is thy sting? O grave, where is thy victory? Oh Jeremy James, where is thy box?"

Jeremy James stepped forward with the box.

"Just put it in the... um... grave, will you?"

Jeremy James put the box in the grave.

"Forasmuch as the souls of these... um... gerbils here departed are in the care of Almighty God," said the Reverend Cole, "we therefore commit their bodies to the ground; earth to earth, ashes to ashes, dust to dust; in sure and certain

...um...possible hope of eternal life, through our Lord Jesus Christ."

Beside the grave was a little pile of earth, which Daddy now pushed over the box until it was completely covered. Then the family went back into the house, and Mummy produced the sandwiches and cakes that were such an important part of any funeral.

"Will the gerbils be in Heaven now?" Jeremy James asked the Reverend Cole, through a mouthful of fruit cake.

"Ah!" said the Reverend Cole, through a mouthful of salmon sandwich. "That's a very good question."

Since he showed no sign of answering it, Jeremy James asked him again.

"Many people do believe that animals have souls," he said, "and if they do, then I'm sure the gerbils will be in Heaven."

"What's a soul?" asked Jeremy James.

"It's the part of you that never dies," said the Reverend Cole. "It's your soul that goes to Heaven."

"Have I got one?" asked Jeremy James.

"Certainly," said the Reverend Cole.

"Where is it?" asked Jeremy James.

"Somewhere inside you," said the Reverend Cole.

Jeremy James would have liked to ask a lot more questions about his soul, but Mummy and the Reverend Cole had to talk about the fete, and so Jeremy James turned his thoughts to fruit cake instead.

That night, Jeremy James couldn't get to sleep. He was thinking about the gerbils and Heaven and his soul. He had asked Mummy and Daddy where his soul was, but their answer had been just as vague as the Reverend Cole's: "Hmmph" (Mummy) and "Worple worple" (Daddy).

He'd also asked them where Heaven was. Mummy thought it might be somewhere beyond the stars, and Daddy thought it was the football ground after a home win.

The problem for Jeremy James was that if the

Reverend Cole was right, and the soul was inside
you, it would have to get out and find its way to
Heaven. How could it do that if it didn't know –
or if you didn't know – where Heaven was? Daddy,
for instance, couldn't even find his way round
London, so how would *he* get to Heaven?

"I expect someone comes to guide you,"
Mummy had said.

And that was keeping Jeremy James awake.
Nobody had come to guide the gerbils. They'd
simply been lying in their cage, then they'd been
put in the liquorice allsort box, and buried under
the apple tree. He would have *seen* if anyone had
come to guide them.

Great-Great-Aunt Maud had been buried on a Saturday. Jeremy James remembered that very well, because Daddy had wanted to go to a football match, and on their way home, they'd had to drive through the crowd. But she hadn't died on the Saturday. She'd died before. So why hadn't she been buried on the day she died?

The answer was obvious. You had to wait till the guide had come before you put the body in the box and buried it. But the gerbils *had* been buried on the day they'd died. And now their souls would be trying to get out of the box and out of the ground before the guide came, because otherwise he'd never find them, would go away, and they would never get to Heaven.

Jeremy James reached for his torch, climbed out of bed, put on his slippers, and opened the bedroom door. The whole house was dark and silent. Everyone was asleep.

Jeremy James crept downstairs, unbolted the kitchen door, and made his way across the lawn to the apple tree.

The following morning, when she looked out of the kitchen window, Mummy was surprised to see a brightly coloured box lying under the apple tree. She knew at once what it

was, and when she went out to take a closer look she found the lid open, and the two gerbils inside, just as dead as ever. She hastily closed the lid, put the box back in its hole, and covered it up.

"I suppose it must have been a dog," she said to Daddy when he came downstairs.

"I shouldn't think a dog would have left them lying there," said Daddy.

But neither of them could think of a better explanation, and they agreed not to tell Jeremy James, because they didn't want to upset him.

Jeremy James didn't wake up till quite late that morning, but as soon as he went downstairs, he wanted to go and look at the gerbils' grave.

"A good thing you spotted it," said Daddy to Mummy, when Jeremy James had gone. "Imagine what he'd have felt if he'd seen them lying there."

When Jeremy James returned, there was a big smile on his face.

"You're looking very pleased with yourself," said Daddy.

And Jeremy James *was* pleased with himself. He knew that the guide had come in the night and taken the gerbils (and the liquorice allsort box) to Heaven. But he decided not to tell Mummy and Daddy. They didn't know enough about souls or about Heaven to really understand.

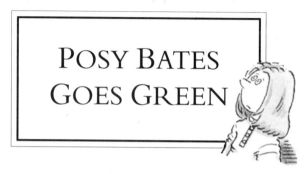

POSY BATES GOES GREEN

Helen Cresswell

"You're not supposed to do that," said Posy Bates, watching her mother spray her newly-set hair.

"Oh no?" You could tell Daff was not really listening.

"No. It goes up in the sky and makes holes in it."

"What? These few puffs?"

"Not just those few puffs. Everybody's few puffs and squirts. They all add up together and make this big hole."

"Well, I have heard that," admitted Daff. "But I don't use a lot."

"And fly spray," Posy went on, "and polish spray and that horrible air-freshener. Pooh – what a stink! That smells nothing *like* fresh air."

"You've got to kill wasps and polish furniture," Daff said.

"Ah, but you can get special squirters," Posy told her. "Pearly says so."

"I'm surprised you ever listen to a word Miss Perlethorpe says," said Daff.

"I don't much," Posy said. "If there's one thing I'm never going to be when I grow up, it's a teacher like her."

"What are you going to be, then?" It was Pippa, come to borrow Daff's hair spray.

"An expert," said Posy promptly. She did not know why she said it. The words just came, as if they had been waiting to be said.

"An expert on what?"

"Nothing. Just an expert."

"You can't be just an expert can you, Mum?" said Pippa. "You have to be an expert *on* something."

Posy cast wildly about.

"Birds and beasts," she said. Those words came out of the blue, too. "Birds and beasts and especially insects."

"Oh – creepy-crawlies!" Pippa was scornful. "You've got spiders on the brain, Posy Bates!"

"Insects are important," Posy told her. "It says so, in my book. We need them."

"Well, I don't, that I am sure of," said Daff.

"Anyway, spiders are better than hair sprays, that I *do* know!" and Posy marched out of the room.

Little did they know that up in Posy's big cupboard there were three caterpillars in a jam-jar waiting to turn into something. She was not sure what.

"Whatever they are, they'll be company for you," she had told Punch and Judy and Peg the Leg.

At least one of them might be a dragon, she rather hoped. She knew that there was not much chance of this, but there was no harm in wishing. If a dragon did emerge, she very much hoped it would breathe fire. This would scare the pants off Miss Perlethorpe and might be useful for cooking. She did not think this fire would be polluting.

Oddly enough, the very next day Miss Perlethorpe announced to the school that there was to be a special event at the end of term.

"A special Green Event," she told them. "We shall plant three trees on the village green, for posterity."

The children themselves were to raise the money to buy the trees.

"You can run errands and do odd jobs," she said. "Or perhaps hold little Bring and Buys. Many a mickel makes a muckle."

"Whatever *that* means!" said Sam Post under his breath.

Posy thought she knew what it meant, and she liked the sound of it.

"Many a mickel makes a muckle," she chanted under her breath on the way home. "Many a pickle makes a puckle. Many a tickle makes a tuckle . . ."

"I shall wash cars to make my money," Sam told her. "What'll you do?"

"Dunno. Haven't decided yet."

Posy went up into her cupboard after tea, to think about it.

"Not something boring," she told Punch and Judy and Peg the Leg. "Not like running errands or washing cars. Something special."

They did not, of course, reply. And it seemed to Posy (even though she could not exactly see their eyes) that they gazed dolefully back at her. It occurred to her that their own lives must be very boring up here in the cupboard, and she felt a pang of guilt.

"I'd better let them out," she thought. "I'd better not collect any more."

The thought was unbearably sad. She was used to their company. She would miss them. They blurred and swam as her eyes filled. Then came the inspiration.

"A Pet Show!"

That was it. She would hold a Pet Show in the garden and charge to come in.

"And you'll be in it!" she told them. "You'll be the most unusual pets there! The rest will be boring old cats and dogs and hamsters. You'll be the stars!"

The spiders and the stick insect showed few signs of excitement, but Posy was sure they had understood.

She spent the rest of the evening making two posters, on the backs of empty cornflakes packets.

"GREAT GREEN PET SHOW. 11 o'clock Saturday morning at 27 Green Lane. Bring your pets. PRIZES for best pet judged by POSY BATES, EXPERT in Birds and Beasts especially Insects. Entrance 20p ADULTS, 10p CHILDREN."

GREAT GREEN PET SHOW

11 o'clock Saturday Morning
at - 27 GREEN LANE
Bring your pets.
PRIZES for best pet
judged by POSY BATES,
EXPERT in Birds and
Beasts especially insects.
ENTRANCE
20p ADULTS,
10p CHILDREN,

She added a picture of a ginger cat with whiskers of an unlikely length, and was satisfied. Next morning she took the posters down to breakfast.

"Never thought of asking me first, I suppose?" said Daff when she saw them.

"I can, can't I, Mum?" Posy begged.

"Oh, go on then," Daff told her.

"Bird and beast expert!" scoffed Pippa.

"But no snakes, mind," warned Daff. "I do draw the line there."

"People in Little Paxton don't *have* snakes, Mum," Pippa told her.

"You never know," said Daff. "You can't tell by people's faces whether they've got snakes."

This, Posy thought, was true. And her mother certainly was scared of snakes. She would scream even if she caught sight of one on television. To be on the safe side, Posy added "No snakes by request", then pinned one poster on the front gate and took the other to school.

"Very nice, Posy," Miss Perlethorpe told her. "It is most original and extremely Green. You may pin it on the wall next to the Window Monitor list."

That evening Posy found some blue ribbon and spent a happy time making it into a rosette. In the middle she stuck a white disc saying "1st Prize".

She looked dubiously at Punch and Judy.

"Ought to be two really, I suppose," she told them. "But the thing is, I can't pin it on you anyway. So what I'll do, I'll just stick it on your jam-jar."

The spiders were asleep, or pretending to be.

"I think perhaps I'll give it to you, instead," she told Peg the Leg. "Yes, that's better. If I give it to two, the others might say it was cheating."

Next day she asked Sam Post to help her.

"You can collect the money," she said.

"I'm bringing my goldfish," he told her. "Bet he'll win."

It was lucky he did not know the judge had already made up her mind. Even if a llama or giraffe turned up at Posy Bates' Pet  Show, first prize would still go to a stick insect.

On Saturday morning the pets started arriving at about ten o'clock. First came Carol-Boot, carrying a wicker basket from which came a lot of mewing and squeaking.

"It's Priscilla," she announced, "and her three kittens. They're called Smudge, Bing and Topsy, and they're bound to win first prize."

"You'll have to open the basket for the judging," Posy told her. "I can't see them."

Not that it would make any difference if she could.

Then came Billy Martin, towing his huge Old English sheep-dog, Ben.

"He's got a pedigree a mile long," he said. "My ma said he could go to Cruft's, if we wanted. He'll win first prize, all right."

He looked scornfully at the dog Mary Pye was leading in.

"We got him from the RSPCA," she told Posy. "His name's Buster. I've trained him to find bits of chocolate and open and shut doors. He bit the postman last week, but it was a mistake. My dad says he's gentle as a lamb."

Buster bared his teeth and growled softly. Posy dropped back a few paces.

"Well, don't let him off his lead," she said. "All dogs to be kept on leads. Ooo – look!"

Vicky Wright came trotting round the house on her donkey, Patch.

"Can I have a ride?" begged Posy.

"All right." Vicky climbed down and Posy got on. It was amazing how high up she felt. The world looked quite different.

"Gee up!" she cried. The donkey did not budge.

"Gee up!"

"He only goes when he feels like it," Vicky told her. "You'll have to wait."

Posy, disappointed, waited. From her vantage point she watched a procession of pets arriving. There were more cats in baskets and cardboard boxes – as least, she supposed they were cats. She certainly hoped they were not snakes. There were mice, hamsters, a tortoise and a whole assortment of dogs.

Miss Perlethorpe was among the last to arrive, leading her white poodle, Selina. She looked about her at the motley assortment of pets and owners.

"Oh, there you are, Posy. Who is organizing? Where is your mother?"

"Inside," Posy told her. "It's my Pet Show. I'm organizing."

"You cannot do that from the back of a donkey," Miss Perlethorpe told her. "*I* had better organize."

She clapped her hands. No one noticed, let alone paid any attention. Posy saw that Ben Briggs' billy-goat had arrived, and was chewing one of the cat baskets – the owner seemed to have disappeared.

"It's a good selection," she thought happily.

"Cats, dogs, tortoises, hamsters, mice, goldfish, spiders, stick insects, budgies, donkeys, goats ..."

She felt that her Pet Show was already a huge success.

"Girls! Boys!" cried Miss Perlethorpe in ringing tones. "Billy – come down from that tree! Come here, everyone, at once!"

Reluctantly her pupils abandoned their games, and gathered round sulkily. They did not expect to be bossed on a Saturday as well as on weekdays.

"Now I want you to form an orderly circle," she told them. "Each stand by your pet, ready for the judging."

They shuffled into an untidy ring. The dogs were now panting and straining at their leashes.

"You are surely not going to judge from the back of a donkey?" Miss Perlethorpe asked Posy. "You must inspect each animal carefully. You cannot do that from up there."

"I can," replied Posy. She did not mention that she had already decided that the blue rosette would go to Peg the Leg. "I can see them all really clearly."

"But what about the cats?" Miss Perlethorpe persisted. "You must come down and look in the baskets."

"Yes, it's not fair!" yelled the cat owners.

"My decision is final," announced Posy. She knew that this was a good remark for a judge to make. "Open the baskets!"

The baskets were opened. So too, it seemed, was Pandora's box. The moment the lids went up, out sprang cats and kittens like jack-in-the-boxes. The dogs jerked their leads from their owners' grasps and were after them in a flash. The billy-goat followed suit and he chased the dogs while the dogs chased the cats. The children, shrieking, chased anything that moved.

Patch the donkey picked that moment to move. Posy had not known a donkey could move so fast.

"Help!" she screamed, as Patch careered through the garden, kicking mouse-cages and boxes left and right.

"Posy, you come back here this minute!" she heard her mother screech.

"Chance'd be a fine thing!" Posy thought.

She could do nothing at all with the donkey, tug

and yell "Stop!" as she might. In the end she gave up and concentrated on not falling off.

She glimpsed dogs, cats, goats in a whirli-gig, and her scampering friends and the horrified face of Miss Perlethorpe. She felt very unlike an Expert in Birds, Beasts Especially Insects. It seemed like hours she clung on for grim life, and when the end of the ride came, she saw it coming.

"No! Oh no!" she screamed, as the donkey headed straight for the little orchard with its low-hanging boughs.

"Here we go!" she remembered thinking, and then the donkey ran straight under an apple tree and Posy was scraped off his back and bump, down on to the tussocky grass.

"Am I alive?" wondered Posy Bates. Then, "Couldn't be wondering if I *was* alive if I wasn't alive, so I must be!"

"You great lunatic!" It was Pippa, panting above her. "You all right?"

"I – think so," Posy said.

"Oooh, you goof! Come on!" Pippa was tugging Posy to her feet, then hugging her. "Honestly, Posy!"

Posy did not get hugged a lot by Pippa.

"She really likes me," she thought happily. "She's glad I'm not dead!"

Daff was next on the scene. For a moment Pippa and she were practically fighting over Posy.

"Oh, thank heaven! Are you sure you haven't got concussion? That donkey ought not to be loose!"

Patch was now aimlessly meandering through the orchard as if butter would not melt in his mouth. In the distance Posy could hear her friends still screaming and dogs barking and, above the pandemonium, the voice of Miss Perlethorpe.

"Go home! Do you hear me? This minute! Every one of you collect your pets and *go home*!"

"Old bossy-boots!" murmured Posy, her face pressed into Daff's cardigan.

"Yes, you take that donkey, Vicky Wright!" she heard Daff say. "And don't bring it here again!"

"Posy could've been dead!" Pippa yelled for good measure. "Wasn't *her* fault she fell off!"

Posy was really rather enjoying all this. Fred was the only one in the family who usually came in for this sort of attention.

In the distance the screams and barking faded, then died away.

"Come on then, love," said Daff. "Are you all right to walk?"

"Dunno," said Posy. Her legs did feel rather wonky.

"You hold on to me," Daff told her.

The trio went slowly back towards the house. Posy's Green Pet Show had disappeared altogether – even Sam Post and his goldfish. Miss Perlethorpe had made a good job of clearing everyone off.

There was not a sign of life, except . . .

Posy caught her breath. There, sitting right in the middle of the patch of grass, and facing her, as if he were waiting for her, was one lone dog. She knew for a fact that he had not been brought to the Pet Show, for the simple reason that she had not noticed him. And this dog, above all others, she would have noticed, because he was, exactly, the dog of her dreams.

His fur was long and black, mostly, though she could see a patch of white here and there. It was so long that she could hardly see his eyes. He stood up. It *was* the dog of her dreams! There were the shaggy legs ending in great furry paws, round and big as saucers.

"Look!" said Pippa. "There's one left. Come on, boy!"

The dog was wagging his tail now, a great waving plume. He advanced, but he was coming not to Pippa, but straight to Posy herself.

"Good boy!" she heard her voice croak. Then she could see his eyes, brown and pleading, and she fell to her knees and buried her face and arms in his soft coat.

"Posy! Are you all right? Oh dear, it is concussion!"

Posy heard her mother's voice as if it were a long way off or in another dimension. She did not exactly *think* "Now, now's the moment if ever I'm to get a dog! This is it! She's so glad I'm not dead she'll give me anything. Now!"

She did not think this, but some instinct told her it was true, though she hardly dared believe it. After years of spiders and stick insects in jars, of hedgehogs and chrysalides, was this warm, furry, solid creature really to be hers? A voice in another layer of her mind was jabbering, "Twice round the garden shed, once round the sundial, clap your hands five times, shut your eyes and say the magic word!" She put a hand in her pocket for the comforting feel of the bag lady's magic bobbin. She mustered all the magic at her command.

When she did finally raise her face it was wet with tears.

"Oh Posy, love," Daff said, "what is it?"

Posy Bates shook her head. For once in her life words would not come. She heard Daff heave a long sigh.

"I can see what's coming," she said. "Come along, then. Better keep it, I suppose, till someone claims it."

And the tears in Posy's eyes were all at once rainbows because the sun, it seemed, had come out for ever. But that is another story ...

MRS BARTELMY'S PET

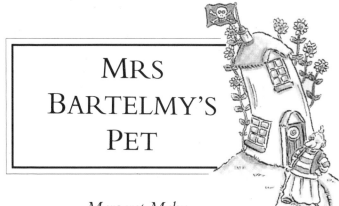

Margaret Mahy

High on a hill in her pointed house lived fierce little Mrs Bartelmy, who had once been a pirate queen. She lived there on her own with her gold earrings and wooden leg, and a box of treasure buried in her garden under the sunflowers.

Though she was fierce, Mrs Bartelmy often felt lonely. She was used to having lots of adventures. She was used to the gay, wicked conversation of pirates. Now she lived on her own she often wished for someone to talk to.

"I could get a cat," thought Mrs Bartelmy, "but they are tame, sleepy animals. I am such a fierce old woman my cat would probably be scared of me. I wish I had been just a granny and not a pirate queen. Then a cat would love me."

Mrs Bartelmy was fond of sunflowers. She planted them all round her house. They grew so tall they

almost hid the roof. One day when Mrs Bartelmy was digging among them she found the biggest cat she had ever seen sleeping there. It was a yellow cat with a small waist and tufted tail, and Mrs Bartelmy liked it at once. It had a golden mane round its face that reminded her of sunflowers. It yawned and showed its red mouth and white teeth. Then it smiled at Mrs Bartelmy.

Mrs Bartelmy went and brought it a big bowl of milk and a string of sausages. The cat lapped the milk. It ate all the sausages and growled fiercely.

"That's the boy!" said Mrs Bartelmy. "I like a chap who enjoys his food. You're fierce enough for me and I'm fierce enough for you. We'll get along together like a couple of jolly shipmates."

At that moment the gate squeaked. Mrs Bartelmy went to see who was coming. It was four men with huge nets and a fat man with a whip.

"We are circus men looking for our lion," said one of the men.

"The wicked, ungrateful animal has run away," said the fat man. "I am Signor Rosetta the Lion Tamer." He cracked his whip.

At the sound of the whip the big yellow cat leaped out, roaring furiously. Mrs Bartelmy's big cat was a lion!

"You aren't to chase this lion," said Mrs Bartelmy. "He's a half-fierce, half-friendly lion and he's my shipmate."

"Well, you could have him," said Signor Rosetta, "but we need him for the circus, and we haven't got enough money to buy another lion."

"Is that all your worry?" said Mrs Bartelmy. She took her spade to a secret corner of her sunflower garden and dug up her chest of pirate treasure. She gave the lion tamer two handfuls of diamonds and Indian rubies.

"Is this enough to buy him?" she asked.

The lion tamer was delighted.

"It is enough to get three lions and two Bengal tigers. Ours will be the fiercest circus in the world!" he cried.

He went away and made the men with the nets go with him.

"That's that," said Mrs Bartelmy. Once the lion tamer, his whip and his nets were gone, the lion became gentle again and smiled at Mrs Bartelmy. It had flowers in its mane and smelled of new hay.

"Well, I never thought to get a cat so much to my liking," said Mrs Bartelmy. "I won't have to worry about scaring it when I get fierce, and it matches my sunflowers."

The lion and Mrs Bartelmy lived happily ever after. Often I have passed them, sitting on the doorstep of their pointed house among the sun-flowers, singing with all their might:

> Oh, there was an old woman
> > who lived on her own
> In a little house made from a smooth
> > white bone.
> And she sat at her door with a
> > barrel of beer,
> And a bright gold ring in her old
> > brown ear.
> And folk who passed by her
> > they always agreed,
> That's a queer little,
> > wry little,
> > fierce little,
> > spry little,
> Utterly strange little
> > woman indeed.

THE PARROT

Italo Calvino

Once upon a time there was a merchant who was supposed to go away on business, but he was afraid to leave his daughter at home by herself, as a certain king had designs on her.

"Dear daughter," he said, "I'm leaving, but you must promise not to stick your head out the door or let anyone in until I get back."

Now that very morning the daughter had seen a handsome parrot in the tree outside her window. He was a well-bred parrot, and the maiden had delighted in talking with him.

"Father," she replied, "it just breaks my heart to have to stay home all by myself. Couldn't I at least have a parrot to keep me company?"

The merchant, who lived only for his daughter, went out at once to get her a parrot. He found an old man who sold him one for a song. He took the bird to his daughter, and after much last-minute advice to her, he set out on his trip.

No sooner was the merchant out of sight than the king began devising a way to join the maiden. He enlisted an old woman in his scheme and sent her to the girl with a letter.

In the meantime the maiden got into conversation with the parrot. "Talk to me, parrot."

"I will tell you a good story. Once upon a time there was a king who had a daughter. She was an only child, with no brothers or sisters, nor did she have any playmates. So they made her a doll the same size as herself, with a face and clothes exactly like her own. Everywhere she went the doll went too, and no one could tell them apart. One day as king, daughter, and doll drove through the woods in their carriage, they were attacked by enemies who killed the king and carried off his daughter, leaving the doll behind in the abandoned carriage. The maiden screamed and cried so, the enemies let her go, and she wandered off into the woods by herself. She eventually reached the court of a certain queen and became a servant. She was such a clever girl that the queen liked her better all the time. The other servants grew jealous and plotted her downfall. "You are aware, of course," they said, "that the queen likes you very much and tells you everything. But there's one thing which we know and you don't. She had a son who died." At that, the maiden went to the queen and asked, "Majesty, is it true you had a son who died?" Upon hearing those words, the queen almost fainted. Heaven help anyone who recalled that fact! The penalty for mentioning that dead son was no less than death. The maiden too was condemned to die, but the queen took pity on her and had her shut up in a dungeon instead. There the girl gave way to despair, refusing all food and passing her nights weeping. At midnight, as she sat there weeping, she heard the door bolts slide back, and in walked five men: four of them were sorcerers and the fifth was the queen's son, their prisoner, whom they were taking out for exercise."

At that moment, the parrot was interrupted by a servant bearing a letter for the merchant's daughter. It was from the king, who had finally managed to get it to her. But the girl was eager to hear what happened next in the tale, which had reached the most exciting part, so she said, "I will receive no letters until my father returns. Parrot, go on with your story."

The servant took the letter away, and the parrot continued. "In the morning the jailers noticed the prisoner had not eaten a thing and they told the queen. The queen sent for her, and the maiden told her that her son was alive and in the dungeon a prisoner of four sorcerers, who took him out every night at midnight for exercise. The queen dispatched twelve soldiers armed with crowbars, who killed the sorcerers and freed her son. Then she gave him as a husband to the maiden who had saved him."

The servant knocked again, insisting that the young lady read the king's letter. "Very well. Now that the story is over, I can read the letter," said the merchant's daughter.

"But it's not finished yet, there's still sóme more to come," the parrot hastened to say. "Just listen to this: the maiden was not interested in marrying the queen's son. She settled for a purse of money and a man's outfit and moved on to another city. The son of this city's king was ill, and no doctor knew how to cure him. From midnight to dawn he raved like one possessed. The maiden showed up in man's attire, claiming to be a foreign doctor and asking to

be left with the youth for one night. The first thing she did was look under the bed and find a trapdoor. She opened it and went down into a long corridor, at the end of which a lamp was burning."

At that moment the servant knocked and announced there was an old woman to see the young lady, whose aunt she claimed to be. (It was not an aunt, but the old woman sent by the king.) But the merchant's daughter was dying to know the outcome of the tale, so she said she was receiving no one. "Go on, parrot, go on with your story."

Thus the parrot continued. "The maiden walked down to that light and found an old woman boiling the heart of the king's son in a kettle, in revenge for the king's execution of her son. The maiden removed the heart from the kettle, carried it back to the king's son to eat, and he got well. The king said, "I promised half of my kingdom to the doctor who cured my son. Since you are a woman, you will marry my son and become queen."

"It's a fine story," said the merchant's daughter. "Now that it's over, I can receive that woman who claims to be my aunt."

"But it's not quite over," said the parrot. "There's still some more to come. Just listen to this. The maiden in doctor's disguise also refused to marry that king's son and was off to another city whose king's son was under a spell and speechless. She hid

under his bed; at midnight, she saw two witches come through the window and remove a pebble from the young man's mouth, whereupon he could speak. Before leaving, they replaced the pebble, and he was again mute."

Someone knocked on the door, but the merchant's daughter was so absorbed in the story that she didn't even hear the knock. The parrot continued.

"The next night when the witches put the pebble on the bed, she gave the bedclothes a jerk and it dropped on the floor. Then she reached out for it and put it in her pocket. At dawn the witches couldn't find it and had to flee. The king's son was well, and they named the maiden physician to the court."

The knocking continued, and the merchant's daughter was all ready to say "Come in," but first she asked the parrot, "Does the story go on, or is it over?"

"It goes on," replied the parrot. "Just listen to this. The maiden wasn't interested in remaining as physician to the court, and moved on to another city. The talk there was that the king of this city had gone mad. He'd found a doll in the woods and fallen in love with it. He stayed shut up in his room admiring it and weeping because it was not a real live maiden. The girl went before the king. "That is my doll!" she exclaimed. "And this is my bride!"

replied the king on seeing that she was the doll's living image."

There was another knock, and the parrot was at a total loss to continue the story. "Just a minute, just a minute, there's still a tiny bit more," he said, but he had no idea what to say next.

"Come on, open up, it's your father," said the merchant's voice.

"Ah, here we are at the end of the story," announced the parrot. "The king married the maiden, and they lived happily ever after."

The girl finally ran to open the door and embrace her father just back from his trip.

"Well done, my daughter!" said the merchant. "I see you've remained faithfully at home. And how is the parrot doing?"

They went to take a look at the bird, but in his place they found a handsome youth. "Forgive me, sir," said the youth. "I am a king who put on a parrot's disguise, because I am in love with your daughter. Aware of the intentions of a rival king to abduct her, I came here beneath a parrot's plumage to entertain her in an honourable manner and at the same time to prevent my rival from carrying out his schemes. I believe I have succeeded in both purposes, and that I can now ask for your daughter's hand in marriage."

The merchant gave his consent. His daughter married the king who had told her the tale, and the other king died of rage.

HOUSE-MOUSE

Ursula Moray Williams

Mrs Melody had no children, no friends, no cat, no dog, no parrot or budgerigar. Mrs Melody lived alone.

When people said "Good-morning" to her, she scowled. When they served her in the shops, she grumbled. When the postman brought her letters, she opened the door the smallest crack to take them in and banged it shut again.

All day long she cleaned her house, wiped the windows, polished the furniture, shone the brasses, and scrubbed the sink. Nobody ever came to see it, which seemed a pity.

Underneath her sink there lived a mouse. He was lonely too. He did no harm in the house. He didn't eat the cheese, he didn't make holes in the wainscot, he didn't leave dirty pawmarks on the shelves. He found all his food out of doo

garden and only came indoors to get some company.

But Mrs Melody didn't like mice. When she caught sight of him she shouted and yelled as if a tiger had come into the kitchen, enough to frighten any mouse away.

But this mouse did not stay away for long because he was so lonely.

In the houses along the road they had cats, and dogs, and noisy children, and terrible mouse traps. He had very nearly been caught in one. So he came back to Mrs Melody and lived under the sink and tried to keep out of her way.

One day Mrs Melody spent the morning dusting everything in the house, using every one of her four dusters. Afterwards she washed them and hung them out side by side to dry on the clothes line in the garden. Then she emptied out the soapy water, but dropped the soap, and when she stooped to

pick it up she slipped and fell headlong, right across the kitchen floor.

She bumped her head on the sink, just where the mouse lived, and out he shot, scared out of his wits, and more scared than ever to find Mrs Melody lying on the floor with her eyes shut.

He ran round and round her. He even tickled her chin with his sharp little nose and whiskers, but nothing would wake her up.

When Mrs Melody did wake up she found she could not move.

"Oh, little mouse! Little mouse! If only you were able to help me!" she said. "If you were a cat you could fetch the neighbours! And if you were a dog you could bark and howl till somebody came. If you were a parrot you could shout: Help! Help! Help! till somebody heard you, but I don't suppose a mouse can do anything at all."

But a mouse could run just as well as a dog or a cat, and at once he ran across the kitchen and out through a crack underneath the door.

He went out into the garden and looked around. On the clothes line Mrs Melody's dusters were blowing in the wind.

Then the mouse had a great idea.

He ran up the post that held the line and began to nibble at the dusters. He bit and he bit and he bit, dropping little mouthfuls of cotton to the ground till the first duster looked like a big H. Then he attacked the next, and nibbled it into an E. The third duster became an L and the last a P.

HELP hung on the line, secured by clothes pegs and waving in the wind.

The next-door neighbour saw it from her window.

"Something is wrong at Mrs Melody's!" she shouted to the lady in the next house, and the lady

passed the message down the street. In a minute everybody was running to Mrs Melody's.

The mouse went indoors and retreated underneath the sink. Soon the doctor arrived and then the ambulance. In less than no time Mrs Melody was whisked away to hospital.

Mrs Melody had broken her leg and it took quite a long time to mend. Everyone was kind to her, and the neighbours brought her sweets and fruit and flowers. Mrs Melody began to smile when she saw them coming, and she also smiled at the nurses and the doctors, and even at the other patients. She became quite a popular old lady in the ward.

"But what we can't understand is how you ever hung that message on the clothes line when your leg was broken!" the neighbours said. "If we hadn't seen it, you might be lying there now!"

"What message?" asked Mrs Melody.

They brought her the dusters and laid them out on her bed.

HELP she read.

"It looks almost as if they had been eaten away!" said the neighbours.

"I believe it was my mouse!" said Mrs Melody.

The mouse waited patiently until Mrs Melody came home.

They brought her one day in a taxi, and now all kinds of people came visiting the house.

Mrs Melody was getting on very well indeed.

She had a bright word for all the visitors that came in, and she always introduced them to her mouse.

He felt a little shy now. There was so much unexpected attention. But when the visitors had gone away, and only he and Mrs Melody were left sitting together in the kitchen, he crept out from under the sink and perched on the edge of the grate, washing his whiskers as he listened to her telling him that he was the cleverest mouse in the world, and she meant to keep the dusters for ever to prove it.

E!G!G!S!

Betsy Byars

The first time I owned a snake I was seven years old, and the snake was mine for about fifteen glorious minutes.

Back then I didn't want to be a writer. I didn't know any writers – I had never even seen one – but their photographs looked funny, as if they'd been taken to a taxidermist and stuffed.

I read a lot, so I saw many dust-jacket photographs, and it seemed to me that no matter how hard authors tried – the men put pipes in their mouths and the women held little dogs – nothing helped. Authors, even my favourites, looked nothing like the kind of person I wanted to become.

This corpselike look, I figured, came from sitting alone all day in a room typing, which couldn't be good for you. Oh, sure, I was glad there were people willing to do this. I loved books and didn't want them to become extinct. But I cared too much about myself and my future to consider becoming one of them.

When I grew up I was going to work in a zoo. I would take care of the baby animals whose mothers had rejected them. I envisioned myself in an attractive safari outfit feeding lion cubs and other exotic off-spring from a bottle.

In preparation for this life my best friend, Wilma, and I played "Zoo" a lot. This consisted of setting up zoos in the backyard and begging people to come and view the exhibits.

The bug exhibit was always the largest but drew the least attention. Ants, doodlebugs, beetles went unacclaimed – even lightning bugs since the zoo was not open at night and their daytime "thing" was resting on the underside of leaves.

Tadpoles (in season) were a popular exhibit, especially when the legs started coming out. Slugs had a certain "yuck" appeal, as did leeches (which we got by wading in the forbidden creek and pulling them off our ankles).

Butterflies were popular, but also seasonal, and the favourite exhibits were the snails and box turtles, which, in addition, required little maintenance.

Admission was free.

Wilma and I were always on the alert for new acquisitions and went about regularly during the summer months turning over stones and rotten logs.

One July afternoon Wilma and I set out, followed by my goat Buttsy who liked to be in on things. While the three of us were rooting through the  woodpile, we came across some eggs. The eggs were buried in the rotten sawdust at the bottom of the pile.

And these were not just eggs. These were E!G!G!S!

We said the word so many times with so many different inflections that it no longer sounded like a word but more like an inhuman cry of triumph.

The eggs were capsule-shaped, about five centimetres long, and leathery in appearance. There were about a dozen of them. They weren't hard like hen's eggs but were elastic and tough. They were light in colour – an almond white – and smooth.

These were really and truly E!G!G!S!

When we calmed down at last, a disagreement followed over what should be done with them.

There were three possibilities.

Wilma brought up the first. She would take them home with her.

I reminded Wilma of the violent reaction her mother had had to our trained cicadas.

This had happened one day when Wilma and I

were training cicadas on her screen porch. This was with an eye to a future circus.

We would start the cicadas up the screen. When they were halfway up, we would tap the screen – sharply – and the cicadas would immediately turn around and go back down. That had been the extent of the training, but we had more complex tricks in mind.

"Get the bugs off the porch," Wilma's mother had said.

"Mom, they aren't bugs, they're cicadas."

"Get – the – bugs – off – the – porch."

"Mom, we're training them."

"Train them over at Betsy's house."

"We can't! Betsy doesn't have a screen porch!"

"Now!"

The second possibility – my own – was that I would take the eggs home with me.

Wilma reminded me of the violent reaction my mother had had to the leeches.

This happened the first time we came upon leeches and didn't know what they were. In our enthusiasm we ran up from the creek to show everybody the weird brown things on our ankles that didn't want to come off.

"Leeches!" my sister had cried in a way that let us know weird brown things were not a good thing to have on our ankles. "Mother, Betsy's got leeches on her ankles!"

My mother came out of the house, got a sharp stick and pried my leeches off. This hurt enough to make me cry. When Wilma heard my cries of pain, she quickly got her own sharp stick and pried hers off herself.

"I don't ever want to see you with leeches on your ankles again," my mother said with a shake of the leech stick.

"You won't," I answered, still tearful.

And she never did because Wilma and I pried the leeches off the minute we got out of the creek, before they had time to stick. The leech display, while not popular with adults, was one of our regulars.

The third, and less appealing, possibility was to leave the eggs where they were.

We compromised.

Wilma put two of the eggs and some sawdust in her mayonnaise jar – the holes were already in the lid. I put two of the eggs and some sawdust in my mayonnaise jar – ditto on the holes – and we left the rest in the wood-pile.

The eggs stuck together a little bit, but we managed to get four separated without breaking anything – including our friendship.

"Be careful! Be careful!"

"I am being careful. You're the one who's not being careful."

The eggs weren't slimy, but they were moist, and Wilma and I promised to water ours faithfully.

We thought – hoped! – the eggs were snake eggs, but we agreed, like future parents, that we would not be the least disappointed in baby turtles.

Wilma's eggs never got the opportunity to hatch because Wilma's sister said, "Motherrrr, Wilma put some funny-looking eggs in our sock drawerrrr."

Wilma had three sisters and they all wore the same size socks and borrowed from each other, so this was not exactly a clever hiding place.

Wilma's mother promptly flushed her eggs down the toilet.

I hid my mayonnaise jar in the back of my cupboard. I checked my eggs often – like two hundred times a day.

About a week after I had put the mayonnaise jar behind my roller skates, one of the eggs looked different. It seemed to move. I took the jar to the window.

A slit appeared in the egg.

Fluid leaked out.

A small snout appeared.

"Everybody! Everybody! My egg is hatching!"

The hatching took about a day. The jar was allowed a place of honour in the centre of the

kitchen table, and we all watched – I with my chin resting on my hands, staring into the glass.

By the time the snake emerged – it took its time – the egg casing had been slashed to ribbons.

The snake was small – about fifteen centimetres in length – and absolutely perfect. It was brownish. My father said it was a bullsnake.

My father held it in his hand and it crawled and twisted in a lively manner. Then I held it in my hand. It was like holding a strand of electrified brown spaghetti.

I dropped it and it got into a perfect striking position. Its tail shook.

My father said, "When a snake wags its tail at you, it's not being friendly."

After that my mother made me put the snake back in the mayonnaise jar, take it out in the yard, and let it go.

"I want to keep it! I have to keep it! I'll take

care of it myself! You won't have to do a thing! I'll keep the lid on the jar! I'll feed it and clean the cage and –"

"Now."

"Motherrrrrrr . . ."

"Now!"

I released the baby bullsnake in the field beside our house. I watched it slither away into the tall grass with the painful, heartbreaking regret that only a seven-year-old who *needs* a snake can know.

Back then, one of the reasons I wanted to become an adult was so that I could have as many pets as I wanted.

My list was long. It started out:

• As many dogs as possible.

• At least two horses – male and female – and all of their colts.

• A goat exactly like my goat Buttsy (who had recently died and whom I missed every time I got in the hammock – Buttsy used to push me).

Now I added to the list:

• Pet snake, preferably nonpoisonous.

THE DUKE WHO HAD TOO MANY GIRAFFES

Fiona Macdonald

Once upon a time there was a duke who had too many giraffes. He was not sure exactly how many he had, but he thought there were about three.

The duke was so poor he had to live in his castle. It was a tall castle on the top of a cliff and every night the wind blew, the sea beat against the rocks and the rain poured through the roof.

The duke did not mind; nor did the giraffes. They were always happy. When it was warm they played games in the sand and helped the duke to make strawberry ice-cream. When it was cold and the wind was singing in the chimneypots, the giraffes sat in the duke's drawing-room and toasted marshmallows. They drank claret while the duke sat in his favourite armchair and told them something of his ancestors. The giraffes did not fidget or ask questions, and sometimes the duke felt so grateful that he would ask them a riddle.

"Why," he would say, "is Sunday like a giraffe?"

Now although the duke always asked the same riddle, the giraffes would shake their heads and look puzzled.

Then the duke, noticing how puzzled the giraffes were looking, would answer: "Because its neck's weak!" Then he would laugh and laugh until he felt so happy he would have some more claret.

Living next door to the duke was a millionaire who had two children. They were called Daffodil and Lief, and they often used to watch the giraffes from the top of an old lighthouse which overlooked the duke's garden. One morning they noticed that the giraffes seemed exceptionally busy. They kept running out of the castle, going to the duke's best cherry tree and removing the ripest branches.

The duke noticed it too.

"Ho, ho," he thought. "Tomorrow must be my birthday, because every year the giraffes make me a cherry cake as a surprise."

The duke had a great number of relations and friends, and on his birthday each year the postman always brought many parcels from them which the giraffes would carry up to his bedroom. So the next morning the duke awoke early and waited for the postman to ring the bell.

But the doorbell did not ring.

"Odd," thought the duke.

He jumped out of bed and went downstairs to see what the giraffes were up to. They were in the kitchen icing the cake.

"Um, I was just sort of wondering," the duke said. "Do you think the doorbell needs a new battery? I mean, sometimes when doorbells don't have new batteries one can be lying in bed thinking of this and that (but mostly birthdays) and never quite realize that the very faint sort of buzzing noise that one couldn't quite hear is in fact a postman with lots and lots of parcels trying to ring the bell. Could that happen, do you think?"

The giraffes, who had been taking it in turns to look over the top of the front door, shook their heads sadly.

"Ah, well," said the duke, sighing bravely, "we'd better have breakfast."

In fact none of the duke's relations or friends had forgotten. Each one had been thinking, "This is the year I shall give him a big surprise." Now all the relations and friends lived far away from each other, and even when they did meet they never discussed birthdays, so none of them knew that they were all going to give the duke the same present. It was not the sort of present that could be posted. It had to be sent either by sea or rail or in very tall lorries.

After breakfast the duke was wondering whether or not to go back to bed when the door-bell rang. One giraffe ran into the hall and looked over the top of the front door.

Standing on the other side was not the postman, but the station-master.

The giraffe opened the door and the station-master said, "Sign this paper here, please. Goods to follow in a moment."

The giraffe, who did not know how to write his name, went back to the kitchen to fetch the duke.

While the duke was being fetched, two strange giraffes walked up the drive. Behind them were another three giraffes and behind them six more. They paused to let a very tall lorry pass them and stop outside the front door. The driver jumped out of his cab and went round the back and opened

136

the lorry door to let out five tired-looking giraffes. As the station-master leant impatiently against the wall, waiting for his paper to be signed, he noticed a large motor boat arriving in the duke's harbour at the bottom of his garden. Onto the duke's jetty stepped three more giraffes.

At that moment the duke came to the door and signed the station-master's paper. "It must be a parcel at last," he said smiling.

Then he noticed that he seemed to be surrounded by strange giraffes, bowing and handing him cards. The duke read a few: "Happy Birthday – thought I'd give you something different this year. With love from Aunt Amnesia." "Happy Birthday. I thought I'd send you something a bit different. Love, Uncle Augustious." "Happy Birthday; something different

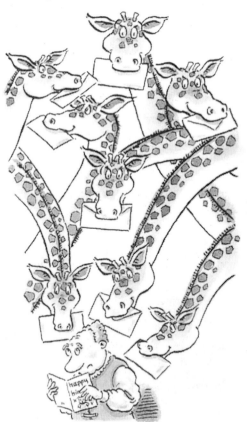

for you this year, from your loving niece Semolina."

"How kind, how kind," murmured the duke, not feeling quite his best for a moment.

He welcomed all the giraffes, gave them breakfast and asked if any of them would care for a bath. When they had all recovered from their journeys, they went into the garden and played games. The duke enjoyed that; it was much more fun with so many. But he was worried. He did not think he could afford to feed so many giraffes. He had only just managed before, but now there would not be enough for all of them.

"I know what," he said. "We could have a fete in the garden to make some money." He told the giraffes and they were delighted.

They helped him to stick up posters in the local town, put up stalls in the garden, blow up balloons and make ice-creams to sell. They also made cakes and toffee-apples and invented competitions.

All this was seen by Daffodil and Lief who had been watching from the old lighthouse. Daffodil and Lief were bored. When they were bored, which was practically always, they used to think of the worst things they could do.

"The duke's having a fete tomorrow," said Daffodil. "He wants to make some money to feed all those ridiculous giraffes."

"So that's what they're up to," said Lief. "I suppose we could make it a bit less boring."

"Yes," said Daffodil, "as soon as it gets dark."

The next day was hot and cloudless.

"It's going to be a great success, I think," said the duke excitedly.

By two o'clock nearly everyone had arrived. The giraffes were putting the ice-cream into cones and they couldn't resist tasting some – but to their surprise it was so salty that they felt quite sick. Then the giraffe unpacking the toffee-apples saw that each one had a large bite taken out of it. Another giraffe who was lifting the cakes out of their tins found that every cake was covered in sand.

The duke was amazed. Who could have done these terrible things? As a diversion he told the giraffes to start the competitions. The crowd did not mind. They played games, ran races, made sand castles and entered the duke's riddle competition. The only trouble was that so many people guessed the answers that the duke had to give away his last bottles of claret as prizes.

Daffodil and Lief had long ago stopped watching the fete. They had made a bonfire on the upper floor of the old lighthouse, using some letters they had found on their father's desk that morning.

"Let's pour this on it to put it out because these flames are getting boring," said Lief, who wanted to empty some liquid from a tin can they had found in the garage.

"All right," said Daffodil.

So Lief emptied the can onto the bonfire. Immediately there were flames everywhere.

"I-I think that was petrol," said Lief, terrified as he saw the floor catch fire.

Daffodil ran to the window. "Help! Help!"she screamed.

None of the people at the fete heard them because they were all laughing so much at the duke's riddles. But two of the giraffes who were on their way back from the cellar with the last bottle did hear and they galloped to the lighthouse.

They reached it just as the flames were about an inch from the children's feet. The children climbed on to a window-ledge and stood there swaying.

The giraffes' heads just reached the bottom of the ledge so the children climbed on to their heads and slid down their necks. When the children had climbed down from their backs safely, the giraffes ran back to the fete, collected the other giraffes who each brought a bucket of sand, and between

them they managed to put out the fire. Daffodil and Lief, shocked, thanked the giraffes and ran home.

The next day the duke was sitting miserably in the drawing-room in his armchair, which he now had to share with two giraffes. They had made no money at the fete since all the things they had hoped to sell had been spoilt.

"Dear giraffes," said the duke, "I really don't know what to do now."

Just then, he heard the sound of something coming up the drive. He looked out of the window and saw a very tall lorry being driven by the millionaire with Lief and Daffodil sitting beside him.

Lief and Daffodil jumped out and ran to the front door.

"My father wants to thank you for saving us, so he's brought you a present," both the children said at once.

The duke, thinking the lorry must be full of giraffes, did not want to look. It was only when he heard the giraffes gasp that he turned round and saw, much to his relief, that inside the lorry was a girafferie.

They put it up in the sunniest corner of the garden and the giraffes went inside it. They liked it so much that they decided they would take it in turns to go to the duke's drawing-room so that he would not have to share his armchair again.

"And," said the millionaire, "I am so ashamed of what my children did to your things for the fete that I'm going to give you enough money to pay for the giraffes' food for the rest of their lives."

The duke was very pleased and thanked him several times.

Lief and Daffodil had been so shocked by the fire that they were never bored again. Nearly every day they either asked the giraffes to tea in the lighthouse or they visited them and brought small presents for the girafferie. The duke grew so fond of each giraffe that he never again worried about having too many, and they lived happily ever after.

WHAT A
DEAR LITTLE
THING!

Dick King-Smith

"Mercy! Mercy!" cried the mouse.

It felt rather a fat mouse, and when Martin removed his paw, he could see that indeed it was.

"Oh dear!" he said. "I'm most awfully sorry!"

Even when the farm kittens were very young, not long after their eyes first opened in their nest in an old hay-filled wooden crib, the mother cat, whose name was Dulcie Maude, had known that Martin was different from his brother Robin and his sister Lark (Dulcie Maude, as you can see from her choice of names, was fond of small birds).

Robin and Lark soon began to have play-fights, leaping upon one another from ambush and pretending to tear out each other's throat with fierce little squeaky growls. But Martin did not like the rough stuff and would hide behind his mother.

And when Dulcie Maude first brought home a very small mouse for the growing kittens, Martin wouldn't touch it. He watched his brother and sister as they worried at the tiny grey body, but he would not join in.

"Aren't you going to try a bit, Martin?" asked his mother. "Mice are nice, you know. What's the matter?"

"It was so pretty," whispered Martin. "Poor little thing."

"Don't be such a wimp," said Robin, with his mouth full.

"You're just a wally," said Lark.

"I quite agree," said Dulcie Maude sharply. "Whoever heard of a cat that didn't like mice!" and she gave Martin a cuff. "Now start eating and stop being so wet!"

Somehow Martin managed a mouthful of mouse. Then he went into a corner and was sick.

And so it went on. Dulcie Maude brought

home more and bigger mice, and, being a no-nonsense mother, insisted that Martin always ate a bit of mouse before he was allowed any of the kinds of tinned meat that the farmer's wife put out for the cats.

All of these – chicken- or liver- or fish-flavoured – Martin liked, but he was made to finish his mousemeat first, and though he learned to keep in down, he could not learn to enjoy it.

Luckily, Robin and Lark always took the lion's share, shoving their wimpish wally of a brother out of the way, and at last the day dawned when Dulcie Maude dumped a final mouse in front of the kittens, and said in her brisk way: "Now then, I've worn my claws to the bone catching mice for you all. You're quite big enough now to hunt for yourselves. You're on your own. See you around."

Robin and Lark were delighted. It was exciting to think of themselves as real hunters, and in barn and byre they stalked their prey or lay in wait, and soon met with success.

Martin was delighted too. It meant that he need never again eat mouse.

Pretty little things! he mused. They shall not suffer because of me. I shall never catch one. But though his intentions were good, his instincts, handed down to him through generations of expert mousers, were too strong, and he caught the very first mouse he met.

145

At the time, he was exploring, in a loft over an old cart-shed. In the days that followed after his mother had left the kittens to their own devices, Martin had done a lot of exploring. Unlike the others, who were always busy hunting, he had plenty of time to wander round the farm. Already he had learned a number of lessons that a farm kitten needs to know.

Cows have big feet that could easily squash you; sows get angry if you go too near their piglets; broody hens are bad-tempered birds; and collie-dogs chase cats.

Humans, Martin was glad to find, didn't chase cats. The farmer paid little attention to him, but the farmer's wife made sure he had enough to eat, and the farmer's daughter actually made quite a fuss of him, picking him up and cuddling him.

One day she took Martin to see her rabbits; three white rabbits with pink eyes, that she kept in three large hutches at the bottom of the garden. Why did she keep them, he wondered?

The next time that Martin met his mother on his journeys, he asked her about this.

"Mother," he said. "Why does that girl keep those rabbits?"

"As pets," Dulcie Maude said.

"What's a pet?"

"A pet is an animal that humans keep because they like it. They like looking after it, feeding it, stroking it, making a fuss of it."

"So we're pets, are we?"

"Strictly speaking, I suppose. Dogs certainly are, always fussing around humans, sucking up to them."

"What about cows and pigs and sheep?"

"No, they're not pets," said Dulcie Maude. "Humans eat them, you see."

"But they don't eat cats and dogs?"

"Of course not."

"And they don't eat rabbits?"

"Yes, they eat rabbits. But not *pet* rabbits."

"Why not?"

As with most mothers, there was a limit to Dulcie Maude's patience.

"Oh, stop your endless questions, Martin, do!" she snapped. "Curiosity, in case you don't know, killed the cat!" and she stalked off, swishing her tail.

It was curiosity, nevertheless, that led Martin to climb up the steep steps into the cart-shed loft to see what was in it. What was in it, in fact, was a load of junk. The farmer never threw anything away, in case it should come in useful one day, and the loft

was filled with boxes of this and bags of that, with broken tools and disused harness and worn-out coats and empty tins and bottles that had once contained sheep-dip or cow-drench or horse-liniment.

Against one wall stood an old white-enamelled bath with big brass taps and clawed cast-iron feet, and it was while Martin was exploring beneath it that something suddenly shot out.

Automatically, he put his paw on it.

"I'm most awfully sorry!" he said again, but the fat mouse only continued to say "Mercy! Mercy!" in a quavery voice. It seemed to be rooted to the spot, and it stared up at Martin with its round black eyes as though hypnotized.

How pretty it looks, thought Martin. What a dear little thing!

"Don't be frightened," he said.

"It is not for myself alone that I beg you to spare me," said the mouse. "You see, I am pregnant."

What a strange name, thought Martin. I've never heard anyone called that before.

"How do you do?" he said. "I am Martin."

What a dear little thing, he thought again. I'd like to look after it, to feed it, to stroke it, to make a fuss of it, just as Mother said that humans like to do with their pets.

After all, he thought, some humans eat rabbits but some keep them as pets. So, in the same way, some cats eat mice, but some

. . .

"Shall I tell you what I'm going to do with you?" he said.

"I know what you're going to do," said the mouse wearily. "After you've finished tormenting me, you're going to eat me."

"You're wrong," said Martin.

He bent his head and gently picked up the mouse in his mouth. Then he looked about him. Then he climbed on to an old wooden chest that stood handily beside the bath and looked down into its depths.

The perfect place, he thought excitedly. My little mouse can't escape – the plug's still in the plughole and the sides are much too steep and slippery – but I can jump in and out easily. He jumped in and laid his burden carefully down.

The mouse lay motionless. Its eyes were shut, its ears drooped, its coat was wet from the kitten's mouth.

"Shall I tell you what I'm going to do?" said Martin again.

"Kill me," said the mouse feebly. "Kill me and have done."

"Not on your life!" said Martin. "I'm going to keep you for a pet!"

A BARN IS A DAYTIME PLACE

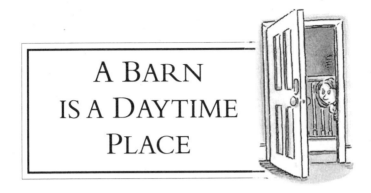

Meindert DeJong

Vestri woke up in the middle of the night. She just had to see the puppies down in the kitchen. But when she ran past Grandpa's and Grandma's bedroom, the door was wide open, the light was on, but Grandpa and Grandma weren't in the room. She and Jon had been sleeping all alone in the house – Grandfather and Grandmother were gone!

Vestri raced back to her bedroom, but Jon was so sound asleep she couldn't shake him awake. She even pulled Jon upright in his bed. But there he sat, eyes tightly shut. Vestri shook him harder, but the moment she let go, Jon dropped down on the bed, still sound asleep. Vestri became so desperate she slapped Jon's cheek.

That slap at last woke Jon. He stared straight up at Vestri and said, "And what do you think you're doing?"

"Grandpa and Grandma are gone!" Vestri said. "The light is on in their room, but they're gone ... Maybe the puppies are gone, too."

Vestri didn't know why she'd said that, but the moment Jon heard it he jumped out of bed. Together they hurried down the stairs to the kitchen. The light was on in the kitchen too, but the puppies were gone – even their bushel basket was gone. Jon and Vestri looked at each other.

"Did they take them back where we got them?" Vestri said, aghast. "Maybe they didn't like them – maybe the puppies kept them awake."

"That's it!" Jon said hopefully. "The puppies kept them awake, so they took them to the barn in the bushel basket. Let's go look."

Vestri hung back at the thought of going to the big black barn in the night. But the house was so empty and still that it was frightening too. She saw a flashlight on the cupboard counter, and gave it to Jon. "Let's go," she urged.

Vestri grabbed one of her dolls that had been on the cupboard counter beside the flashlight, and ran after Jon. Behind him she stepped out of the lighted kitchen into the pitch-black night.

"Wait for me," she begged. "Please!" But she didn't feel safe until she'd grabbed the waistband of Jon's pyjamas. She clung to it.

"Man, Vestri," Jon scolded in a hushed, hoarse voice, "don't be so scared."

"But I am scared," Vestri gasped. She clung to her doll with one hand; with the other hand outstretched she clung to Jon. She followed him closely across the yard.

Suddenly the flashlight shone its small pinpoint of light through the enormous hay doors that stood wide open, into the big black cavern of the night barn. But wherever the flashlight ranged, the floor of the barn between the two huge haymows towering to the peaked roof was empty. Outside, the night lay dark and still. Inside the barn, everything was dark and still.

Suddenly there was a small sound in the stillness. It even scared Jon, until at last he whispered, "That was just the cows in the basement."

It wasn't the cows. It was Grandpa! He suddenly came up from the basement. He saw Jon with the flashlight. Vestri stood so close behind Jon, Grandpa did not see her.

"Are you looking for me?" Grandfather said. "I'm looking for Grandma, but she isn't in the basement. Possibly she's up in the haymow. Hey, that flashlight's a good idea – let's have it."

But to climb to the haymow Grandpa had to turn off the flashlight. As the light disappeared Grandfather seemed to rise up in the darkness – straight up in the air. It turned out to be the ladder leading to the hayloft. Grandfather started up the ladder. Jon and Vestri climbed up after him. Vestri scrambled so hard after Grandpa that at times she grabbed his heels instead of the rungs of the ladder.

"You're supposed to climb the ladder, not me," Grandpa said from up in the hayloft. Then he reached down and pulled Vestri up, and after her he pulled Jon up into the hay. He turned the flashlight over a huge mound of hay. At first hay was all they could see. Then behind a mound of loose hay appeared a pair of big eyes, blinking into the light. It was Grandma!

"What – what are you three doing here?" she asked.

"Looking for you," Grandpa said.

"And the puppies," John added so loud that it rang and echoed under the high roof beams of the barn.

"Yes, the puppies," Vestri said.

"Oh, my goodness," Grandma said. She tried to sit up, but the loose hay kept slipping and sliding from under her. "I built the sides of our nest too high," she laughed. "But I didn't want the puppies to climb over and fall down to the floor of the barn."

Grandpa, Jon and Vestri waded through the deep hay to Grandma. There she lay in a deep nest of hay with only a white pillow for her head and a shawl thrown over her nightgown. It was lovely and warm in the new-mown hay high up under the roof of the enormous barn.

Next to Grandma in a little row lay the puppies. They were snuggled so cosily and sleeping so deeply after the excitement of their big day, they didn't even hear all the talk above them.

Behind Grandma, at the back of the hay nest, stuck down in deep dents, stood three small, white, empty bowls.

Vestri was almost crying at the awfulness of Grandmother's sleeping in the big dark barn. "Grandma, why are you sleeping here?"

Grandmother laughed. "Well, I'll tell you. There was no sleeping in the house with those three wailing puppies. They were crying high and low. One would start mournfully low, the next one would go higher, and the third one would shrill out higher still.

"But worst of all were the three of you. The puppies woke me up, but they didn't wake any of you. Their noise disturbed your grandfather just enough that he started rolling and thrashing and snorting. It got so bad that I had to put one hand on the floor to keep from going overboard. Then when the puppies stopped a bit to rest their throats, I could hear you two children. Jon must have been dreaming about that squawking heron, because he kept laughing so loud he sort of sounded like the heron. And right in the midst of the laughing, it sounded as if you, Vestri, were reading a long Sunday school lesson to your dolls."

"No Grandma!" Vestri and Jon said almost together.

"Yes, Grandma!" Grandmother said. "And you three sleepers were the ones who wanted the puppies in the house. Well, I went down to the kitchen and made myself a cup of coffee and tried to keep the puppies quiet, but finally I told them, "Sitting up all night is no fun for any of us. Why don't we all get some sleep?"

"So I threw a pillow on top of their basket, for me, and I put my old woollen shawl over my shoulder, dumped three little bowls in with the puppies, and then we went to the barn. First we went down to the basement where the cows were, because I thought the puppies had yammered themselves hungry. The new cow kindly gave us three bowls of warm milk, so we had a little milk party right here in the barn. When they had lapped all their milk, they were so warm and so sleepy that I dumped them all back in the basket and tied it over my shoulder with the shawl, climbed the ladder, dug a deep nest, and there we were – sound asleep until you three came blundering in."

"Hey," Grandfather said, "that is an idea! It's high time you two city children found out what fun it is to sleep in a barn in the new-mown hay. I'll get us some pillows and we'll join Grandma."

Vestri and Jon looked a little doubtful, but they said nothing.

Grandpa disappeared down the ladder and with him went the only light. Vestri snuggled as close to Grandma as possible. Jon sat down and whispered, "Oh, the hay is warm and soft, Vestri. It tastes sweet, too."

He was chewing a stalk. It was the only sound in

the barn until Grandma said sleepily, "It sleeps the way it tastes – you'll see. Hay sleeps sweet."

That is how it was in the morning. They slept so sweetly, so soft, so long, the people and the puppies, that the sun seemed a great red ball rolling in through the wide-open doors of the barn. It was the cool of the morning, but the whole barn was sweet and warm with hay. They all sat up and looked out of the doorway – out over the fields. Then, far away in the rose-red of the morning, the blue heron flapped down from the sky to the blue water of the lake.

They looked at each other and then down at the puppies, and almost together they breathed deeply and said, "Ah." At that sound the puppies woke up.

"Ah," Grandpa said. "Now we'll feel like living again through another day. Ah."